Midsummer Madness

A Lord For All Seasons
Book 2

Nadine Millard

ARE YOU SIGNED UP FOR DRAGONBLADE'S BLOG?

You'll get the latest news and information on exclusive giveaways, exclusive excerpts, coming releases, sales, free books, cover reveals and more.

Check out our complete list of authors, too!

No spam, no junk. That's a promise!

Sign Up Here

www.dragonbladepublishing.com

Dearest Reader;

Thank you for your support of a small press. At Dragonblade Publishing, we strive to bring you the highest quality Historical Romance from some of the best authors in the business. Without your support, there is no 'us', so we sincerely hope you adore these stories and find some new favorite authors along the way.

Happy Reading!

CEO, Dragonblade Publishing

Additional Dragonblade books by Author Nadine Millard

A Lord For All Seasons Series
A Springtime Scandal (Book 1)
Midsummer Madness (Book 2)

Prologue

"MY DEAR MRS. Templeworth, I must tell you again how wonderful Elodie has been. Why, the children simply adore her."

Hope Templeworth rolled her eyes as she settled in to listen to yet another resident of Halton wax lyrical about her paragon sister.

It wasn't that she envied Elodie the praise. Hope would rather stick pins in her eyes than adhere to the implacable rules Elodie imposed on herself to be the perfect Society miss.

But Elodie was a tough act to follow. There was no doubt about that.

Mrs. Bell, the vicar's wife, went on and on about whatever new, wonderfully giving act Elodie had just committed while Hope looked around the quiet streets of their village and tuned her out.

She spotted Francesca leaving the small bookshop, her hands full, her nose already buried in whatever weighty new tome she'd purchased.

Francesca was terribly clever. It was rather intimidating, truth be told.

Though she was no bluestocking, Cheska was fierce and bright with a spine of steel.

Their younger sister Sophia had run off somewhere. No doubt spotting a horse or a dog or a cat that she wanted to pet.

Heaving a sigh, Hope looked around again, nodding and smiling at those who called greetings. She wasn't oblivious to the appreciative looks she was getting.

From infancy, when Elodie was called good, Cheska was called clever, or Sophia adventurous, Hope was called pretty.

And for the past few summers, she'd been hearing it more and more. Noticing it in the furious blushes and hesitant smiles of the young men in their village.

It wasn't exactly something she was proud of, but she supposed it was better than nothing. Some area in which she wasn't compared to her sisters and found lacking.

Mrs. Bell and Mama drew to the close of their conversation and said their goodbyes.

"Gooday, Miss Hope," the vicar's wife said kindly if a little stiffly. Hope had never gotten the impression that Mrs. Bell particularly approved of her. "And might I just say how fetching you look in your new spencer? Pink is so becoming on you."

Hope smiled her thanks. The dusky pink was perfectly nice against her caramel curls and brown eyes. But it was also beautiful on Elodie, Cheska, and Sophia. Or it would be if Sophia would be caught dead wearing something so feminine.

Cheska sidled up and slipped Hope the book she'd requested, a novel that Mama would ardently disapprove of.

"Here," she whispered. "Don't forget you said I could read it before Elodie."

"I won't forget," Hope said. "Cheska, do you think it's odd that nobody ever compliments me on anything other than how I look?"

Cheska ran an eye over her.

"Not really," her brutally honest sibling said. "You know how these things go. A pretty smile, a mop of blonde curls, and nobody really wants anything else from you."

"But you're blonde," Hope objected, a little stung by the words but not really knowing why. "And beautiful. And Elodie is beautiful. Sophia, too, come to that. Yet people at least talk about some other traits you have."

"Oh, your lot in life is *so* terrible." Cheska grinned. "Imagine the hardship of being the most beautiful girl in the world."

Hope shoved her sister's shoulder, then stumbled when Cheska shoved her right back.

"You're only sixteen," Cheska continued her ribbing, but Hope knew it was in jest. "Plenty of time for you to grow a brain."

"Thank you," Hope bit sarcastically. "How wonderful of you to say so."

"At least you don't look like the back of one of Sophia's horses," Cheska countered. "Count your blessings."

Hope stuck her tongue out, and they bickered back and forth on the way to collect Sophia from wherever she'd wandered to.

But she still felt a little uneasy.

Perhaps Cheska was right, though.

There were worse things in the world than to be considered a pretty face.

She should just count her blessings.

Chapter One

Four years later...

HOPE SIGHED AS she dipped her legs into the cool water of the lake.

The summer heat was stifling, the sun beating down on her unrelentingly.

It had been worse in London, she supposed.

At least here in Halton, there was the opportunity to find shade in the trees of the orchard on their estate. Or hide under the canopy of the folly near the lake. Or this, hitching her skirts up and removing her stockings and shoes, allowing the blissfully cool water to lap against her calves.

She was contemplating stripping off her gown altogether and going for a swim, but she knew her mother, who was already annoyed that she'd just left her third Season with no fiancé, would likely have a tantrum about her unladylike conduct, and she'd rather not have to listen to it.

It wasn't that she hadn't received offers. Indeed, for the last three Seasons, she'd received so many proposals that Francesca, Sophia, and even Elodie had started taking bets on how many she'd actually get before she accepted someone.

The problem, Hope thought to herself, was that not one of them held even a flicker of interest for her.

Not one of them had ever attempted to engage her in any real conversation.

Everything was about how pretty she was. They wrote poetry dedicated to her hair, her eyes, or her smile. But none of them had ever asked her an opinion on anything.

They told her of their wealth, their sprawling homes, their excellent connections. But they never wanted to know if she had interests of her own.

In short, every one of them wanted her for what she looked like and nothing more. Truth be told, most of them probably didn't even know what she sounded like, so disinterested in actually listening to her were they.

Her mother didn't think any of that was important. Especially since Elodie's marriage to Viscount Brentford two years ago had ensured the girls were now in the same circles as peers of the realm and the upper echelons of the ton. But it was important to Hope. She wanted a husband who at least *liked* her and not just what she would look like on his arm.

And while Francesca had said in no uncertain terms that she would not be marrying until she was desperately in love or firmly out of options, and maybe not even then, Hope didn't share her eighteen-year-old sister's dislike for marriage as an institution. She just wanted someone to want her for *her* and not for her hair, eyes, smile, or any of the other nonsense those insipid poems referred to.

Was it so bad to want someone who didn't bore her to tears? Someone who might even be a challenge?

The truth was that from the time she'd been in long skirts, she'd had the admiration and devotion of nearly every member of the opposite sex that she'd come in contact with.

Indeed, her sisters had often utilized that particular trait— because it wasn't a skill really—to their advantage when they were hatching some scheme or other.

It had been Hope who'd charmed Lord Brentford's staff two years ago while Elodie had stowed away in the man's carriage. And Hope who'd helped the viscount when he'd fallen in love with Elle, and almost lost her.

And only last year when Sophia had spotted a dog being mistreated by a local farmer, Hope had flirted shamelessly with the man while Sophia had kidnapped it.

Flirting had become second nature to Hope. Fluttering her lashes to get her way was *au fait*. So commonplace that it was tedious at this point. It made no difference if it was a country curate or a dashing duke. They were ultimately all the same.

But she would have to pick someone, she knew. Next Season she would be twenty-one. High time to find a man to settle down with. And even more importantly, high time to get out of this backwater town and live a little.

Maybe she'd become one of those marvelously sophisticated Society wives who carried on scandalous affairs behind their husband's backs. She could pick one of the rich gentlemen who offered for her and then while away her life spending his money and eyeing up his footmen. She wouldn't be the first woman to live such a life. And truth be told, people probably half expected it from her anyway.

Though she'd never fallen into true scandal or ruin, everyone who knew her knew of her flirtatious nature, and she walked a fine line between what was acceptable and what would get her family snubbed.

Elodie used to despair of it, but thankfully her marriage to Christian had made her a lot less stuffy.

Mama still despaired of it. Vocally. Especially since now that Elodie was married, Mama had to chaperone her girls herself and not rely on her eldest daughter to take the brunt of the responsibility.

Papa, in all honesty, didn't notice his children one way or another.

But even though she couldn't imagine herself loving any of the dandies she attracted during the marriage mart, she still didn't want that sort of life. She didn't want to be that sort of wife.

She wanted to at least care about the man.

And she was absolutely sure that she'd marry.

Unlike Cheska, Hope didn't think she had very many options open to her as a woman.

It was either marry or be a spinster.

So surely the least she deserved was a husband who could hold her interest for longer than five minutes.

Feeling frustrated with the direction of her thoughts, Hope decided that the heat must be making her more maudlin than usual.

And then deciding that it was worth Mama's wrath, she stood and made light work of removing her white muslin gown and her stays.

She threw her straw bonnet on top of her clothes, then un-pinned her curls, allowing her hair to fall down her back.

With a quick look around to make sure she couldn't be seen, she waded into the lake until she was deep enough to dive under the cool, clear water.

The cold was blissful against her heated skin, and she swam further into the lake, relishing the silence and the coolness.

When she needed to take a breath, she pushed up off the silty bottom, then lay back to float on the water's surface.

Her chemise was by now completely see-through and cling-ing to her skin, but she cared not a whit. It was glorious and freeing to be swimming practically naked on a hot summer's day. What harm was she doing in any case? There was nobody around to see her.

Hope had no idea how long she lay there floating, her mind wandering, the water lapping against her rapidly cooling skin. But when she started to shiver from the cold, she righted herself and then swam until her feet hit the sandy bottom of the lake.

Standing, she tossed her now-sodden tresses over her shoul-ders before turning toward where she'd left her clothing in a heap.

She looked up and the smile dropped from her face.

Standing at the edge of the lake was the most sinfully hand-some man she'd ever seen.

And he was looking straight at her.

Chapter Two

G IDEON BELL, EARL of Claremont, stood frozen in place as he watched a beautiful woman emerge from the lake like something from a fantasy.

He had no idea who she was or how he'd stumbled upon her, but he sure as hell was glad he had.

He watched her toss her hair, and his mouth dried as his eyes raked over an incredible body, wrapped in the transparent material of a cotton chemise.

If he were a gentleman, he would of course turn away, or at least alert her to his presence. But truthfully, he couldn't remember a time anyone had accused him of being a gentleman, and he had no intention of earning that title now.

He spied a bundle of clothing near his feet and knew they must be hers.

And that meant that she was heading right this way. In that clinging, soaking wet undergarment.

Gideon wanted to drink his fill, but his damned conscience awoke at the most inopportune time. He might not be a gentleman exactly, but he wasn't voyeuristic. And he might be stunned by this lady of the lake, but he wasn't a complete bastard either.

So, he decided, he'd have to sacrifice that incredible view in deference to the lady's modesty.

And he was just about to turn around. He truly was. But

suddenly she stopped, and her eyes darted to his face.

And he was frozen once more.

Those eyes, big, deep brown pools in the middle of a heart-achingly beautiful face. The mouth, pink and plump and opened now in an 'oh' of shock. He watched, fascinated by a pink blush that traveled across her cheeks, her neck, and lower still...

He expected her to scream, or cry. Maybe even faint. Certainly, cover herself up in shame and panic. But to his amazement, and great delight, she raised an eyebrow and held his gaze, tilting her chin up mutinously.

"If you're going to hang around here, might you make yourself useful and hand me my gown?"

She was Quality. If her finishing school accent hadn't confirmed it, the way she held herself like a queen would have.

But there was a glint in her eyes, mischievous and playful. She was trouble.

Gideon's guess was that she was well aware of her beauty and the effect she had on men.

And he had no intention of being one of her admirers, of which there were many, he had no doubt. At least not obviously. Keeping his face perfectly smooth, he bent and picked up the perfectly modest white gown at his feet.

"Do you usually strip off and swim in public?" he asked.

There was a husk of desire in his voice, but it was no matter. She'd never heard him speak, so she couldn't guess that it was there because he was so affected by her.

"Of course not," she responded aghast, the very picture of ladylike outrage. And then, that glint. "Only when I'm sure there's an audience."

Gideon felt his jaw drop at the chit's audacity. He'd never known a gently bred lady to be so, so playfully forward.

Then again, he hadn't known that many gently bred ladies, truth be told. At least not in any way that really mattered.

"But I think that's enough for today's performance, so if you wouldn't mind turning your back?"

One of her hands kept the gown covering her body, as though he hadn't seen it. As though every luscious curve wasn't indelibly imprinted in his mind. The other, she lifted so she could indicate turning with her finger.

"Do I get to know your name, Lady of the Lake?"

Rather than giggle like a dimwit, which he'd half expected, she snorted.

"Hmm, I rather think I prefer the title you've bestowed upon me. Adds a touch of intrigue to our unfortunate situation."

"Unfortunate?" he asked, knowing she couldn't see his smile but unable to keep it from his face.

When he'd agreed to come and stay awhile with his uncle in this sleepy little hamlet, he hadn't expected to find anything remotely amusing about the place. And certainly nothing as vastly interesting as a half-naked beauty bathing in a lake right in front of his eyes.

"I wouldn't say that," he continued.

"Well, you wouldn't, would you? You're not the one practically naked in front of a stranger."

She was outrageous.

Never in his life had he met a woman comfortable with talking in such a fashion unless she was firmly established in the *demi-monde* or lower.

And this lady, for all her outlandishness, was most definitely not *demi-monde* or lower.

"That's easily rectified," he continued, feeling a bit ridiculous but finding her intriguing enough to continue. "Not the stripping off part, unless that's what you want, of course?" Her deafening silence told him what he thought of that particular idea. Shame. "But if you give me your name, and I give you mine, we'll no longer be strangers."

"Ah, but where is the fun in that?"

Her voice was soft and husky, and damned if he didn't feel it slide seductively over his nerve endings.

"I'm decent," she continued airily, and Gideon turned back

around to face her.

"Decent" was perhaps a stretch, and the way she looked made him feel perfectly *indecent.*

The dress didn't do much more than her chemise to protect her modesty since it, too, was white and was now clinging to her still-wet skin.

He could no longer see the tantalizing glimpse of her breasts, so he supposed she *was* more decent but not by much.

She wrung out her hair before flipping it over her shoulder, then bent to retrieve her stockings and shoes.

"Well then, I should be on my way. It's been a pleasure, sir." She grinned, dimples that he suddenly longed to lick making an appearance on her lovely face.

No, not lovely.

Beautiful. She truly was absolutely beautiful.

Just who on earth was she?

Gideon had no clue, but he had every intention of finding out.

"The pleasure has been all mine, my lady. Trust me."

Her deep brown eyes sparkled at his words, but she shrugged, looking for all the world as though she heard similar sentiments every day. She probably did, come to that.

But was that an ever so slight pink tinge in her cheeks?

Before he could study her skin, well, all of her really, she turned and skipped off through the fields, barefoot and looking like she hadn't a care in the world.

Should he think her improper? Scandalous? Offensive?

Perhaps.

Though he'd be the utmost hypocrite if he did since his own behavior since boyhood had been less than stellar.

When he found himself still staring though she had long disappeared, he turned in the direction of the vicarage.

His uncle was retiring, and Gideon's younger brother was taking over as reverend. Gideon had offered Kit the living at Claremont, but Kit's stubbornness wouldn't allow him to accept.

Apparently, he was determined to stand on his own two feet, as it were.

When their uncle had written and told them of his plans to retire to Bath, offering Kit the living in Halton, the younger man had jumped at the chance. And given what the brothers had just lived through in Claremont, Gideon had agreed to join him for a while.

Perhaps a month or two spent in Halton would help to clear some of the awful memories of Claremont, of his father, of Elaine…

Feeling his memories drag him down a dark path, Gideon determinedly cleared his mind of thoughts of home.

Kit had had some business to finish up in Town, and because Gideon had no desire to see the Season limp to a close in London, he'd decided to travel ahead of his brother and get here a few days early.

Hopefully, by the time he returned to Claremont for the harvest as he planned, he would have moved on from all the ugliness that had occurred last year.

He glanced back at the pond, the water glistening in the afternoon sunshine. And despite the maudlin turn of his thoughts, he couldn't suppress a quick smile.

His arrival in Halton had felt like a colossal, boring mistake.

But now, well, maybe it wouldn't be so bad.

Chapter Three

"Lord, Mama. I have no intentions of visiting the new bloody vicar, even if he is Old Bell's nephew."

"Watch your language and your manners, Hope Templeworth."

Hope gritted her teeth at Mama's shrill condemnation.

"You are the eldest here now that Elodie has married, and as such, you must do your duty. We must welcome the new reverend. How would it look if we didn't?"

"It would probably look like we don't care about the new reverend. Which we don't. At least I don't. Why can't you take Francesca?"

"Because it is not Francesca's duty. And I cannot join you today in any case. I have a meeting with Mrs. Thompson about the orphanage. Mrs. Bell's loss will be felt keenly by our committee, and we must make sure we have planned for it accordingly."

"Wait, so I'm to go alone? Absolutely not."

Mama's face started to turn red. Always a sure sign that one of her daughters had upset her. Not exactly a shocking turn of events, but inconvenient all the same.

"Hope. You will go. You will pay our respects. You will bring this basket." Her mother lifted a basket filled with various treats and breads Cook had made that morning. "And you will welcome Mr. Bell to Halton as is befitting a man of his station and a family of ours. His brother is an *earl,* for goodness' sake. An earl!

Though Mrs. Bell says he's been traveling the continent for some time now, it's still an excellent potential connection."

Hope scowled at her mother, but she knew there was very little point in arguing.

Cheska would flatly refuse to go, Hope knew, especially if she heard Mama's talk of connections. Sophia couldn't be tracked down from sunup to sundown and was too young regardless. So that left her.

Not for the first time, Hope wished Elodie and Christian had decided to settle here in Halton for no other reason than Saint Elodie would have happily tripped off to meet the new vicar in town.

Hope couldn't wait for them to visit for a spell when they quit London before traveling to Christian's main seat in Hampshire. Because while Hope could think of nothing more boring than an afternoon of polite chitchat with a man of the cloth, Elodie would happily do so. Perhaps even enjoy it. And Christian was always just happy to be wherever Elle was.

Although, Hope frowned at the basket dumped in front of her, at least it would get her out of the house for a bit.

She was the first to admit that she'd been hiding away since her encounter with that mysterious stranger at the lake. Even now when she remembered his black eyes boring into her, the half-smile on his lips, the breadth of his shoulders as he'd peered down at her, her whole body broke out in gooseflesh.

She'd been mortified to have been caught practically naked by a strange man. Of course she had. Despite what some might whisper about her, she wasn't a hussy. But she'd brazened it out because what else had there been to do, really? Cry? Faint? She wasn't the crying, fainting sort.

Besides if her sisters ever got wind that she'd behaved in such a ninnyish fashion, she'd never live it down.

Yet underneath the embarrassment, there'd been something else. Something dark, and exciting...and wicked.

Hope knew that fear should have been front and center in her mind. They'd been quite alone, and she had been as vulnerable as it was possible to be. Yet, he hadn't scared her. He'd intrigued her.

Casually mentioning him this morning at breakfast had yielded no information about him. Mama hadn't heard of a new arrival beside the new vicar who wasn't due until the end of the week. Nor had Sophia. Cheska didn't care, and Papa wouldn't have noticed.

But not an hour ago, Mama had torn through the house screeching for Hope. The vicar, Mama had gasped, had arrived early, leading to this demand for Hope to do her familial duty.

For one wild moment, Hope had thought Mama had meant her mysterious stranger. But that was ridiculous of course. Flirting shamelessly with a half-naked woman was certainly not the behavior of a vicar.

But she had no time to extrapolate further, for Mama was well and truly up in the boughs about the new Reverend Bell and how he needed a visit *immediately*. And now, hours later, Hope was about to give in.

"Fine," she complained, throwing her unbound hair over her shoulders. "I'll go and see the paragon himself. But I warn you, he mightn't be too happy with me. I'm not Elodie, you know."

"No, you're not," Mama snapped. "If you were more like your sister, perhaps you, too, would have caught a peer for a husband."

Hope scoffed. Not only because she'd received no less than five proposals from peers this Season, but because Christian had fallen in love with the Elodie who'd stowed away in his carriage, run away from him when he'd displeased her, and if Hope's suspicions were correct, had most definitely *not* acted the virtuous paragon with her now-husband. It had been Elodie's less-than-perfect behavior that had won Christian's heart.

Not that Hope could blame her sister. There was no doubt that Christian was positively scrumptious.

Her mind flashed back to the man at the lake.

Sable hair, eyes dark enough to look almost obsidian in the summer sun, and scrumptious probably wasn't an accurate word to describe him. Darkly, dangerously handsome was more fitting.

"Hope?"

Hope dragged her gaze back to Mama.

"Sorry, I stopped listening," she said, brutally honest and unbothered by Mama's scowl.

Mama's sigh sounded like it came from the depths of her soul, but it had no effect on Hope because she was used to it. They all were. They'd been hearing it since infancy. Except Elodie.

"Be sure that you stay long enough to be polite," Mama warned her, a glint in her eyes. "Do not think I've forgotten when you spent your visit to the magistrate in the stables with his servants."

Hope grinned, despite Mama's obvious displeasure.

The servants to which Mama was referring had been vastly more entertaining than the fat magistrate and his annoying wife.

"I will stay for no more than fifteen minutes and no less than ten." She smiled at her mother with faux sweetness.

She loved her mother, she did. But saints above, the woman could be difficult.

Mrs. Templeworth glowered at her suspiciously before nodding.

"Very well, I shall be back for dinner. Put your hair up. And take a maid."

Hope heaved a sigh, then grudgingly went in search of a bonnet. She hated wearing her hair up, but it wasn't worth the argument.

It was far too warm for a spencer or pelisse, so she left her sky-blue walking dress uncovered, only stuffing her hair under a straw bonnet with a blue ribbon to match her gown, not bothering to pin it.

Then, snatching up the basket, she set out for the rectory on the other side of Halton.

She should probably take the gig, but by walking, she could

delay the visit.

Passing Sophia in the stables, Hope found Francesca reading on the rope swing they'd hung from a giant oak as children.

"Cheska."

Francesca didn't even look up from her book, keeping her blue eyes trained on the pages as she flipped them over, her blond hair falling over her face.

"My answer is no."

"You don't even know what I was going to say." Hope scowled.

"No, I don't. But Mama was looking for you earlier and so, whatever it is she asked you to do that you're now trying to drag me into, my answer is no."

"You're a terrible sister."

"Tell me something I don't know." Francesca smiled up at her, then dropped her head again.

Hope huffed, then turned toward where Sophia was putting her favorite mare through her paces.

"Sophia?" she called.

Before she could say another word, Sophia turned to glare at her, her chestnut plait flying over her shoulder.

"Absolutely not," she shouted back.

"Ugh. You can both go to the devil," she yelled and then stomped away, wishing that she could be anywhere but here.

Well, she thought as her mind inevitably drifted to her encounter with the stranger, and the embarrassment she'd felt under his scrutiny, *here and perhaps the lake.*

Chapter Four

GIDEON ROLLED THE tumbler in his hand, staring into the contents as though the brandy would hold the answer to moving on from the wreck his life had become.

He'd been alone with his thoughts all morning since his uncle and aunt had gone off on their various errands. Retiring to Bath apparently required a lot of goodbye meetings.

This place, this town, was all a bit too close-knit for Gideon's liking. But Kit would enjoy it. He'd probably love the small-town community where everyone knew each other, and everyone knew each other's business.

That was not for Gideon. Not in the slightest.

Hopefully, the gossips here wouldn't get hold of Kit's business.

How could their family ever hope to explain the circumstances around his father's death? Kit's desire to leave home? Gideon's constant sense of guilt around the whole damned thing?

Far better for things to remain their sordid little secret. It wasn't as though his father or Elaine could tell anyone now in any case.

Sighing in frustration at his maudlin thoughts, Gideon threw back the contents of his glass before refilling it.

It was far too early to be drinking this much, he knew. His uncle wouldn't approve, though he wouldn't say much about it. Not only because Gideon was funding a sizeable chunk of the cost of the move to Bath, but because his uncle was good to his core, unlike Gideon's father, and simply wouldn't berate or criticize his nephews.

Having never had children of their own, his aunt and uncle had doted over Gideon and Kit as boys. As they'd grown into men, Gideon had seen less of Aunt and Uncle Bell, but Kit had remained close to them. Their uncle was a big part of why Kit had wanted to become a man of the cloth. And it made sense that Kit would be the one to take over this flock.

Unbidden, an image of his lady of the lake popped into Gideon's head, and despite his somber mood, he couldn't hold in a smile. Somehow, he didn't imagine the bold beauty would be a well-behaved, saintly sheep. Kit would have his work cut out when he arrived at the end of the week.

Gideon had been wondering who she was since the day of their brief encounter but having had luncheon just this afternoon in the only inn in Halton, he had a suspicion.

Surely, she must be one of the much-talked-about Templeworth girls. All afternoon he'd heard them spoken about. Sometimes in tones of reverence, sometimes fear. Most times a mixture of fondness and exasperation.

And through it all, there was talk of Miss Hope. Miss Hope, who'd smiled at one man, batted her lashes at another. Miss Hope, who was more beautiful than the sunrise, lovelier than a winter's morn.

They were a poetic lot; he'd give them that.

But surely this incomparable beauty had to be the woman who'd been haunting his dreams these past few nights? There couldn't be two such beauties in one small town.

Although if he were to guess, he'd say all the Templeworth girls were quite beautiful if the dazed looks on the faces of the local lads were anything to go by. Still, this Hope character was definitely something special, by the sounds of it. He'd been tempted to question the serving girl about these Templeworths. Thankfully, though, common sense awoke, and he stayed silent.

But he'd kept an eye out for her like a dolt on the walk back to his uncle's house all the same.

The sound of a caller echoed toward where Gideon was hiding in his uncle's modest library.

"Damn and blast," he whispered to himself.

The last thing he wanted was to spend a painfully polite thirty minutes with one of his uncle's many parishioners.

If he was in one of his own properties, he'd just ignore them. But he couldn't be rude for the sake of Kit, if not his aunt and uncle.

Sighing, he got to his feet, donned his charcoal superfine, and quickly retied his cravat. Then he stood with his hands behind his back, every inch the perfect gentleman, waiting to endure the company of whoever came through the door.

A subtle knock signaled the arrival of the ancient housekeeper, who still stammered and stuttered around him, even though he'd always been unfailingly courteous.

A mistress had once told him he looked monstrous when he didn't smile. She'd meant it in a good way, but he didn't imagine Mrs. Fetherson being as enamored of that quality as his mistress had been. And he'd had little cause to smile in the last few months.

"Miss Templeworth to see you."

Surely not! Had he been thinking of the chit so much that he'd managed to conjure her? Perhaps it was a sister.

"Of course," he said when he realized the woman was awaiting an answer.

The housekeeper bobbed a curtsy, then stepped back.

It was her.

His lady of the lake. Dry today but still heart stutteringly beautiful.

He watched her face closely, wondering if she'd recognize him.

She did if her sudden gasp and the widening of those incredible eyes were anything to go by.

Gideon took his time raking his gaze over her. His memory hadn't done her justice. The glorious curves that had imprinted themselves in his brain were covered today in a pretty blue dress that was somehow almost as tantalizing as the wet chemise given the way it skimmed her hips and hinted at her generous breasts.

Her hair was covered in a fetching bonnet, but he glimpsed enough renegade tendrils to see that when it was dry it was the color of a light, golden caramel.

Once again, his mouth dried as he took her in.

For her own part, her eyes flickered with shock, then heat, then bizarrely something akin to disappointment before she smiled.

"If it isn't my mystery man," she quipped saucily and despite his dark, tumultuous thoughts of only moments ago, Gideon felt his own lips pulling up in an answering grin.

"If it isn't my lady of the lake," he nodded.

"Ahem."

The less-than-subtle cough alerted Gideon to Mrs. Fetherson's now-disapproving presence.

"Ah, Mrs. Fetherson, perhaps some tea for our guest?"

The old lady ran a squinting glare between Gideon and Miss Templeworth before leaving to do his bidding.

"So, you're Reverend Bell's nephew?" she asked, and it might have been Gideon's imagination, but he thought she sounded disappointed by the fact.

"I am," he said. "Gideon Bell. And you are Miss Templeworth. My guess is you are Hope."

Her grin was pure devilment.

"An excellent guess. Are you also some sort of magician?"

He snorted softly. "I'm afraid it's nothing so interesting. I just have excellent hearing."

At her frown of confusion, he elaborated. "Your sisters and you seem to be the talk of the village on a regular basis."

He thought she might blush, but she merely shrugged, magnificently unperturbed.

"Well, it's a small town. They don't have much to talk about."

Gideon remembered his manners and offered her a seat, waiting until she perched herself on the chaise before taking a seat on the armchair opposite her.

"How did you know which one I was?" she asked curiously.

"Ah, that was easy. Every male within a five-mile radius sounded utterly besotted. Who else could it be?"

Instead of simpering or giggling behind her hand, she rolled her eyes.

"Lord, don't tell me you've managed to charm poor, unsuspecting ladies with that tosh!"

Gideon barked out a laugh, rusty from lack of use over the last few months.

"I can't say I've ever had to work that hard to charm a lady, Miss Templeworth. But I assure you, 'tis true. You are quite the most beautiful woman I've ever encountered, dry or wet."

Gideon wondered how innocent the woman standing in front of him was. He watched carefully to see if she'd pick up any innuendo in his comment, but her face remained clear of any sexual knowledge.

So, all that sensuality was natural then, and not the product of experience? His stomach twisted with a sudden jolt of desire. He could only imagine what she'd blossom into when in the right hands.

"Thank you," she answered wryly, not seeming the slightest bit impressed or flattered. "But my sisters are just as pretty, I assure you."

"I doubt it," he answered honestly. "But I look forward to meeting them."

"Why? So you can try that stuff on them? I can assure you, Cheska wouldn't be remotely impressed. She is something of a detractor when it comes to men and marriage. And Sophia is only sixteen." Her eyes flashed, and he didn't know if she was jealous or simply overprotective of her siblings. "And Elodie is married," she continued. "She is Viscountess Brentford."

Gideon was indeed familiar with Brentford. They belonged to the same clubs and had attended Oxford within a couple of years of each other. He'd even met the viscountess, and now that Hope mentioned it, he could see a familial similarity. Though the viscountess was a brunette, her eyes were similar to Hope's.

However, he still maintained that while the viscountess was beautiful, and Christian was damned lucky in his choice of wife, the woman in front of him was superior in beauty and had wit and vivacity that only added to her attraction.

Best to keep that to himself, though. Since she seemed to think his genuine flattery was poppycock.

"I am familiar with the viscount and your sister," he answered evenly, and she blinked in surprise. "And I can assure you, I will not make any attempt to be charming to your sisters."

"I didn't say you couldn't try, just that it wouldn't work." She grinned, dimples appearing on either side of that delectable mouth.

"So, do you often visit gentlemen alone?" he asked with a raised brow.

She narrowed her eyes at his false innocence.

"I do not," she sniffed. "It just so happens that I very properly brought a maid currently ensconced with Mrs. Bell's cook, who is her aunt. Besides, how much harm could there be in visiting a vicar?"

She said the word with a vague disgust.

"I brought this," she announced suddenly, and he noticed a basket that he hadn't even glanced at before. "To welcome you to Halton, apparently."

"To welcome *me?*" he frowned as he accepted the basket. "My thanks to you."

"It's not from me," she answered. "I mean, it's not just from me. My mother wanted me to welcome you officially. From our family. Officially."

He couldn't help but grin at her frown, a confusion that clearly matched his own evident on her face. Then she smiled, and he literally caught his breath at the beauty of the expression. He didn't think that happened outside of books and plays.

"Truth be told, I'm not very good at all this. Elodie was the proper, ladylike one. She would have known exactly what to say. How to act. I'm unfortunately rather lacking in that area."

Gideon couldn't stop himself from looking her over once more.

"I can't imagine you lacking in any area, Miss Templeworth," he said, his voice gravelly. "And ladylike behavior is highly overrated."

He was being far more risqué than he would usually be with a debutante, but there was something about Hope Templeworth that awoke his less-than-gallant side.

He wondered if he would offend her by his forwardness, but she didn't seem fazed in the slightest.

"On that, we can agree," she said drolly.

Just then, a maid entered with a tea tray and placed it on the table between them.

"Shall I pour?" Miss Templeworth asked, suddenly all demure politeness.

"Of course," he answered smoothly while trying to figure her out.

For someone who claimed to be lacking when it came to polite society, she certainly knew what she was doing. She poured like a perfectly bred young lady and only that constant glint of mischief belied her true personality.

"I think your mother taught you rather well, Miss Templeworth." He nodded his thanks as he took the delicate cup from her. "That was very well done."

Truth be told, he hated tea. Couldn't stand the stuff. But it was one of those ridiculous quirks of polite society to drink it, so he did.

"I'm not without some skills," she answered innocently, but his body raged as though she'd propositioned him.

What the hell was this? This incendiary desire? He hadn't felt even a flicker of interest in the female sex since Elaine and her betrayal. So why was he sitting here remembering Hope Templeworth practically naked, and wishing quite fervently to know if she tasted as good as she looked?

Chapter Five

H OPE TRIED TO ignore the flicker of awareness that crackled around her as she sat across from Mr. Bell. Just as she tried to ignore the disappointment she'd been feeling since she'd set eyes on him in the rectory.

The new vicar was her mystery man from the lake. How dreadfully boring.

Even now as she sat here taking tea with him, she couldn't quite believe that this darkly handsome man could be a *vicar*. He was too masculine, too dark, too sinful.

The way his lips quirked while he said things that no vicar she'd known would ever say. The way his dark eyes devoured her. The way he watched her as she imagined a panther would watch his prey…

How could a man like this be a man of the cloth? How did he not scare the wits out of his pious parishioners?

There was a power about him, innate masculinity that was frankly wasted on a life of religious devotion. He exuded power and something else, something primal and exciting and wicked that she'd never encountered before. All of that just to give sermons on Sundays? It was a shame. Such a shame!

Her flirtatious comment about her skills probably fell on deaf ears, too. The innuendo was lost on a man who no doubt only saw the good and proper in everyone and everything. Yet, he hadn't seemed all that good and proper himself the other day by the lake. Just remembering the heat in his dark gaze set Hope to blush.

"So…" A change in subject seemed prudent. "Are you looking forward to meeting more of your new community at the party?"

Reverend and Mrs. Bell were hosting a dinner party to welcome their nephew to Halton next Thursday. Hope had told Mama that she'd rather stick pins in her eyes than attend. Now, she wasn't so sure. Even though Mr. Bell was a vicar, she was still more fascinated by him than anyone she'd ever met.

From his grimace, he was as happy about the dinner party as she was, though he kept his face smooth as he nodded.

"Of course," he answered evenly. "I'm looking forward to seeing if you dance as well as you swim."

Hope felt her cheeks heat but prayed it didn't show too much on her face. The last thing she needed was for a bloody vicar to think she was attracted to him. Even if she was.

She didn't know quite what to say in answer. If he weren't a reverend, she would have happily given him a flirtatious answer. But really, of all the ladies in the world, the last one to have any sort of relationship with a man of the cloth was Hope Templeworth!

"My brother will be excited to meet everyone," he said smoothly when she didn't answer. He was frowning slightly as though he was confused by her silence, and she couldn't blame him, really. But it was long past time that she got their acquaintance back on an even, respectable keel.

"Your brother? He is coming to stay, too?"

Mr. Bell looked at her like she'd grown another head.

"Er, yes," he answered. "It would be rather imprudent for him to stay away would it not?"

Now it was Hope's turn to stare at him. Why would it be prudent for his brother to be here? And why was he looking at her like she was a complete dolt? She was growing more confused by the second.

"I'm sure it will be a great comfort to you to have your brother's support. Though the rumor was that he was abroad."

"Abroad? His support? For what?"

Hope could only stare at him in consternation. Was the man addled in the head? It certainly seemed so. She was about to answer when the drawing room door opened with a bang and Reverend and Mrs. Bell swept into the room.

"Miss Templeworth. How nice to see you," Mrs. Bell said weakly, and Hope knew that it very much *wasn't* nice for the prudish Mrs. Bell to see her.

If Elodie had been here, Mrs. Bell would have been delighted to see her sister. Would have pressed her to accept a dinner invitation and chatted for hours about things almost guaranteed to put anyone *but* Elodie to sleep.

"A pleasure to see you, too, Mrs. Bell," Hope lied smoothly, using the arrival of the older couple to jump to her feet. "But I'm afraid I've stayed as long as I can. Welcome once again, Mr. Bell, to Halton. I shall see you all at the party. Good day."

Without giving any of them a chance to respond, she practically ran from the room.

"IT'S FUNNY WHEN you think about it."

"It is decidedly *not* funny."

"It's sort of funny."

Hope glared at her two sisters, wishing she'd never run home and blurted out the whole sorry tale to them. They were taking far too much delight in the fact that the mysterious gentleman Hope had sighed over was, in fact, a do-gooder of the highest order.

Against her better judgment, she'd been fantasizing about seeing him again. In the woods perhaps. They'd talk, they'd flirt. He'd gaze at her, barely concealed passion in those black-as-sin eyes…

Just like in the novels she gobbled up.

None of those novels, not one of them, had had the dashing, brooding hero be a vicar.

"Perhaps he's a sort of rogue vicar," Cheska offered unhelpfully. "I can't imagine Reverend Bell flirting with a practically naked woman in a lake. Can you?"

Hope shuddered at the very idea.

"That is disgusting," Sophia spat. Which it was. "Besides, even if he was a *rogue vicar,* he'd still bore Hope to tears. She's always going on about how she can't wait to get out of Halton."

That was true. She *was* always going on about it because she *was* desperate to get out of this small town. Not desperate enough to have tied herself to one of those inane dandies from Town of course. But still. Quite desperate.

"Well, perhaps this brother of his will be as dashing *and* infinitely more exciting," Cheska said by way of cheering her up, Hope supposed. She merely smiled weakly in response, not wanting to admit the truth to her sisters. That she couldn't imagine any other man having that strange, exciting effect on her. "And he's an earl. You'd get an entire year out of Mama not haranguing you if you bagged an earl, Hope."

All the Templeworths considered Hope to be their romantic. But to admit that one meeting with a stranger had convinced her she'd never again be attracted to another man? They would mock her mercilessly. Probably cart her off to Bedlam for good measure. And she would deserve it.

"Well, it's of little consequence in any case," she said stoutly. "I have no intentions of getting involved with a vicar *or* his brother. Now, Sophia. Have you decided what gown you will wear to the party?"

Just as she'd intended, Hope's question immediately brought about a cessation to the talk of Mr. Bell and her very inconvenient attraction to him.

"Ugh, no I have not," Sophia scowled, her eyes narrowing.

"Because as I've told you *all,* I'm not going."

Hope's sigh matched Francesca's.

"You have to go, Sophia," Hope said. "You know this. You're lucky that you got to sixteen without being dragged into this sort of stuff, to be honest. I was only fifteen when I was forced to endure these things."

"Yes, well that's your own fault for looking like a China doll," Sophia bit out as though Hope had any control over how she looked. "I look like I belong in the stables. Which I do."

Francesca rolled her eyes.

"All you're being asked to do is stop dressing like a man for one evening and endure some polite company. Even you can manage that, Sophia."

"I don't *want* to manage it."

Lord! They were all stubborn, but Sophia definitely got the lion's share of that particular trait.

"Hopefully Elle and Christian will arrive early., Mama won't care a whit if I attend or not once her golden viscountess is in town," Sophia said hopefully.

That was true, actually. Hope might even get out of it if Elle and Christian arrived.

"She'll probably still make you go. The reverend is a single man, after all. I don't think even Christian's being a peer can prevent Mama's scheming."

"I would rather *die,*" Sophia, not usually prone to dramatics, shuddered.

"She's too young for him," Hope snapped at the same time.

Francesca turned her attention to Hope. "Is she? I doubt Mama would give two hoots about his age. How old is he, anyway?"

Hope shrugged, feigning a *nonchalance* she was far from feeling. The very idea of her mystery man and Sophia…

"How should I know? We're hardly friends."

"But you know enough to know he's too old for Sophia?"

"Sophia isn't interested," the brunette interjected. "Bloody hell. If a viscount for a son-in-law isn't enough for Mama, we're all doomed."

If Elodie were here, she would likely scold Sophia for her language. But Hope couldn't be bothered, and Cheska was rather a big fan of swearing.

"I don't know," Cheska said casually to Sophia, though that piercing gaze stayed on Hope's face, watching carefully. "If you married the handsome vicar, you could stay in Halton with your horses. You wouldn't even have to suffer through a Season."

"Oh, now that's something to consider," Sophia looked up from where she'd been brushing muck from her breeches.

"She's not marrying the vicar," Hope snapped.

Then without another word, she marched from the room.

But not before she caught the smugly knowing smirk on Francesca's face.

Chapter Six

"THIS PLACE AND the people in it are mad, Kit. Stark, raving mad. You're quite sure this is where you want to hang your hat for the rest of your days?"

Kit laughed at his older brother's harsh assessment of Halton and its residents.

He'd arrived late last night, and the brothers hadn't had much time to talk between helping their aunt and uncle prepare for their retirement, and Aunt Bell's fussing over Kit the same way she'd fussed over Gideon when he'd first arrived.

"I think I could be quite happy here," Kit said before picking up his tankard of ale and draining it. "I don't seek constant adventure and excitement the way you do, Gideon. I never have."

That was certainly true, Gideon mused as he raised a hand to signal for another two pints.

And for all its faults, Halton did have good ale.

It also had a great view of the bustling village square from the table he'd steered Kit toward. Not to look out for a particular blonde with deep brown eyes, he assured himself fiercely, but because Kit would want to see village life. To get a feel for this place and his flock.

"No, I don't suppose you have," Gideon responded after the blushing serving girl had taken her time placing the tankards on the table between them. He didn't miss the blatant invitation in her eyes any more than he missed the generous curves she did little to cover up.

Kit, being the unending gentleman, had averted his gaze.

"So, are you looking forward to your party then?"

Kit laughed at Gideon's obvious displeasure. "Well, clearly you're not," he quipped.

He was always so jolly. So *nice*. Even after everything that had happened. Even after Elaine's betrayal. Their father's betrayal. His own betrayal.

Gideon's stomach churned, and he brutally pushed the memories away. If Kit didn't blame him, then he could learn not to blame himself.

"You know a country dance isn't exactly the top of my list on how to enjoy myself."

"And none of the local ladies have caught your attention?"

Gideon immediately thought of Hope Templeworth, who had more than caught his attention but had then acted for all the world like he'd gravely disappointed her and then ran off.

He hadn't seen her since.

Well, perhaps it was just that she was insane as the rest of them.

Kit was chattering away happily, as though the ugly heaviness of their family's shame didn't rest on his shoulders the way it did Gideon's. And Gideon was fiercely glad that his bright, younger brother hadn't been so adversely affected by Elaine's betrayal that it changed who he was at his core. Someone good. Someone kind. Someone who cared enough for others to dedicate his life to helping them.

Someone who…

His thoughts froze as his gaze found the woman who'd been occupying his mind for the past few days. Damn, but her beauty was beyond compare. He'd never seen the likes of it anywhere in the world.

He remembered how enamored of Elaine's raven hair and big blue eyes he'd been. But they were nothing to the golden-haired, doe-eyed loveliness that he gazed upon now. It caught him by surprise every time he saw her.

"What is that? A procession of some sort?"

Kit's question had Gideon dragging his gaze from Hope to her surroundings. He scowled in response to what he saw.

A procession indeed. A procession of lovesick puppies followed her around as though she were handing out treats as she walked. Gideon gritted his teeth, surprised and annoyed by the surge of jealousy.

Beside her was another blonde—beautiful, too, though she didn't have that same enticement as her sister. He presumed they were sisters because there was a likeness between them. And because he'd heard so many tales of the incorrigible Templeworth girls to know they traveled in packs.

Indeed, there, bringing up the rear, a chestnut-haired beauty in the first throes of womanhood. He couldn't stifle a smile as he watched her march over to her sisters, dressed in breeches and clearly unbothered by what a scandalous image she presented.

But he only spared a moment's glance for the sisters. His eyes were inevitably drawn back to his lady of the lake.

"Gideon?"

He realized that he'd been ignoring his younger brother while he'd been salivating over the blonde across the square, no better than her entourage of sycophants.

"Not a procession," he answered, his voice gravelly. "Just the undeniable effect of Hope Templeworth."

He saw Kit's frown of confusion from the corner of his eye but damned if he could tear his gaze away from the chit.

She had a hold over him. There was no explaining it. No denying it. To himself, at least. And he wouldn't speak a word of it to Kit, knowing full well that he'd sound insane to be obsessing about a woman he'd spoken to twice.

"Ah, Aunt Bell wasn't as charmed by the lady as the gentlemen out there seem to be."

That caught Gideon's attention, and he turned to his brother.

"What do you mean?" he asked. Demanded, really.

Kit blinked at the biting tone.

"I inquired after the family who'd left the welcome basket. I wanted to make sure that I offered them my thanks appropriately."

Of course he did, Gideon thought wryly. Ever the perfect gentleman.

"And she told me not to become 'ensnared' by the Misses Templeworth. Especially Miss Hope, she said. Not the type of company a vicar should be keeping."

Gideon couldn't contain his oath, whispered though it was. He loved his aunt but to hear that she'd been disparaging Hope... Well, it bothered him. Likely far more than it should.

"I told her she didn't have anything to worry about, of course," Kit continued oblivious to Gideon's darkening mood. "Though truth be told, now that I see her..."

"Aunt Bell was right," Gideon suddenly cut in, forgetting that only seconds ago he'd been thinking quite the opposite.

But hearing Kit salivate over Hope was more than he was willing to put up with. Kit turned to stare at him, and Gideon met his gaze, keeping his face carefully smooth.

"Trust me, Kit. A woman like that would destroy a vicar."

"A woman like what? She sounds wonderful."

Both Kit and Gideon turned at the sound of the husky voice that addressed him.

And there she was. A vision in lemon and white.

Gideon stood slowly, Kit almost leaping from his seat across the table.

And because Gideon was watching Hope's face so closely, he saw the flicker of hurt in her huge, brown eyes. She knew he'd been speaking of her.

Yet, it was true, wasn't it? A vicar, a gentle soul like Kit, would never be able to keep up with her. And she'd be bored stiff within two days. She was far too vivacious, far too witty and bright for someone as dull, albeit kind-hearted, as Kit.

He realized that Hope was awaiting a response, realized that Kit was awaiting an introduction, his face flushed, his eyes slightly dazed. Something he was coming to learn was common in young men around Miss Templeworth.

"She is," he said softly now. "Quite wonderful. As I think she well knows."

Her brow rose in response to this, and Gideon couldn't contain his smile.

"Miss Templeworth, may I introduce my brother, Kit? Your new…"

"Kit? It's *so* good to meet you. Welcome to Halton. I hope you'll find everything and everyone to your liking."

Gideon narrowed his eyes as Hope batted her lashes at his poor, woefully under-equipped brother. Indeed, Kit's cheeks grew alarmingly scarlet in the face of such blatant flirtation.

"I do hope that you will be staying with us for a time, as I am sure you must be exhausted from your travels. My sisters and I are always happy to make new friends."

Kit's jaw popped open, but Gideon was both suspicious and confused. She hadn't once glanced at him, and her comment about Kit's travels and staying for a time made no sense.

He glanced past her to see her two sisters eyeing him speculatively, the elder squinting slightly, the younger running her gaze insolently from his Hessian's to his hair and back to his face.

"Well, she wasn't wrong. He *is* rather beautiful, if a bit rough around the edges."

Gideon felt his brows rise in surprise, and he turned his attention fully to the blonde and brunette running critical eyes over him.

He was growing accustomed to Hope's forthrightness. And he'd certainly heard enough about the incorrigible sisters. But to see young ladies so uncaring about the strictures of society, well, it was unusual. But certainly refreshing.

"Hmm. Far too old for me though, she was right about that."

Gideon covered his choke of shock with some coughing.

What the hell had they all been saying about him? And why in God's name had his name, his age even, been mentioned in the same sentence as a girl barely out of childhood? The thought was disgusting.

"Please allow me to introduce my sisters."

Gideon's attention was caught once more by Hope's sultry tone, and he turned to frown at his brother who was ogling the sassy blonde with stars in his eyes. Utterly besotted in mere seconds.

I know the feeling, Gideon thought wryly.

"My sisters, Miss Francesca Templeworth and Miss Sophia Templeworth. Ladies, his lordship, whose title I'm afraid we've yet to learn," she dimpled at Kit who was still looking rather dazed, then threw a dismissive glance Gideon's way. "And our soon-to-be Reverend Bell."

For a moment, Gideon thought she was offering him some sort of slight by not using his title.

But even as he scowled at her, the pieces slid into place.

The odd comments, the surprise about his brother, the vague air of disappointment after the veritable fire between them at their first meeting. She thought he was the bloody vicar!

Gideon didn't know whether to feel amused or insulted. He'd never been accused of being anything *close* to a man of God in his life. And he would love nothing more than to show the seductive Miss Templeworth exactly why that was.

But a kernel of mischief awoke in him. And when Kit's confused frown cleared, and he opened his mouth no doubt to set Miss Hope to rights, Gideon found himself grasping his slighter brother's shoulder.

"A pleasure, ladies," he smiled at the brash Templeworth girls. "I do hope you will be joining my brother and I at the rectory for the party two days hence. It is sure to be an interesting evening."

Without giving the beautiful sisters a chance to answer, or Kit the chance to voice any of the confusion stamping his brow,

Gideon manhandled his brother to the exit.

Childish, perhaps. But he couldn't help it. Hope Templeworth had roused his interest more than any woman he'd ever met. And his interactions with her had made him smile when he'd thought nothing would.

It was far too tempting to play this little game with her.

He now knew that her stilted behavior around him had been because she thought him a vicar. But unless he was very much mistaken, the attraction he felt was returned. Perhaps not to the same incendiary level, but certainly to some point.

Clearly, the idea of his being the new reverend displeased her. For a moment, Gideon's gut clenched uncomfortably. Was a vicar not good enough? Was she determined to marry well? Marry wealth or a title? Just like Elaine had been…

He knew it was probably unfair to assume all women were as mercenary as Elaine, but he couldn't help it. Would Hope Templeworth ignore any attraction between them now? Or would she be tempted by him, even thinking him only a vicar?

Chapter Seven

"CHRISTIAN MIGHT HAVE some competition, you know. That man is positively scrumptious."

Hope scowled at Francesca and Sophia as they began an in-depth discussion of who was more handsome, their brother-in-law or the new vicar.

Though Christian was indeed almost obscenely handsome, he didn't have that raw, brooding appeal that Gideon did. Not to her at least. Elodie would likely argue otherwise.

But Gideon. Hope had thought there was an edge to him, something dark. Something that spoke to a wickedness in her that she'd never quite been able to quash. Not that she'd ever tried, truth be told. To know she'd been mistaken, that he was the very opposite. Well, it was acutely disappointing, and her sisters' chatter wasn't helping her bad mood.

Scowling did nothing to stop Cheska and Sophia from shamelessly listing the qualities of both men, so Hope ignored them, choosing instead to stew on what Mr. Bell had been saying in the inn.

They'd only been in there because Sophia was chasing down Laurence Townsley, who had promised her a look at his new pair of grays, and she'd refused to go home until she'd found him.

When they'd entered the inn, Hope had immediately spotted Gideon and the shorter, slighter man she'd guessed was his brother. And when her first instinct had been to turn tail and run, she'd forced herself to march over to their table, refusing to be cowed by a man. A *vicar*.

Hearing what he'd thought of her, that she would destroy him, had been a tad hurtful. Not because she had any romantic interest in him. Of course, not that. It was just hurtful.

But then he'd said she was wonderful… Or perhaps he hadn't been talking about her at all.

Hope huffed out a sigh, annoyed by her circuitous thoughts. Disappointed that his brother hadn't, in fact, turned out to be an even more godlike version of him.

Though perfectly polite and nice, Kit Bell had seemed the shy and sensitive sort. Much more suited to the life of a small-town reverend in Hope's opinion.

She felt the beginnings of a headache press against the back of her eyes.

"I suppose, all things considered, it really comes down to the size of their…"

"Francesca!"

Hope wasn't usually the sister discouraging such talk, quite the opposite in fact, but for some reason, she didn't want her sisters comparing Gideon's *anything* to Christian's.

"What?" Cheska asked innocently, though there was a bite in her eyes that told Hope her sister was trying to bait her. Before Hope could snarl at her, which she very much wanted to do, the stables of their home came into view.

"He's here!"

Sophia's shout rent the air, and Hope looked to see who the "he" was.

Not Christian, who stood grinning in the middle of the stables. But his stallion, Mercury, with whom Sophia had been smitten for two years now.

"Hello to you, too." Christian grinned indulgently as Sophia barged past him and began murmuring to the stallion, stroking his jet-black coat, and altogether ignoring the viscount towering over her.

From Hope and Cheska, he received a nicer and more polite welcome.

In fact, they'd come to love their brother-in-law, forgiving him for hurting Elodie only two years past. It was easy to forgive when Christian made his adoration for his wife so obvious.

"Where is Elle? I hope you're here for at least a couple of weeks. It will keep Mama's focus off us," Cheska said, not giving the viscount a second to actually answer her questions. "And you must join us for the Bells' party, of course, to welcome their nephews, one of whom is to be the new vicar. If you're wondering which one he is, just look at the man who is positively *made* for sin. He'll be the one Hope is making moon eyes at."

Hope glared at Cheska's retreating back as her sister dashed off toward the house.

Steeling herself for Christian's curiosity, for the viscount was as bad as the old biddies at Almack's for gossipmongering, she glanced up into his cobalt stare.

"A vicar, Hope?" he asked in faux amazement.

"Oh hush," Hope snipped. "You should know better than to listen to Cheska's nonsense."

Christian raised a brow, the picture of disbelief.

"Truly," Hope insisted. "Do you honestly think I'd show an interest in a *reverend*?" She made sure to arrange her face in a mask of distaste.

"No," Christian conceded. "I can't picture it. And truth be told, I would have thought Claremont was more your type."

"Claremont? That's the earl?"

"Indeed. I didn't think he was back from Europe. I haven't seen him in Parliament in an age."

"He seemed a little old for the Grand Tour," Hope said, wanting to talk about Gideon and therefore stubbornly continuing the conversation about Kit.

"Far too old for a year of carousing," Christian agreed with a crooked smile. "But there were rumors of some sort of family fallout. The old earl passed quite suddenly, if memory serves. And there was a to-do around the man's betrothed. Or the vicar's betrothed. I can't remember the details, in all honesty."

Hope didn't know if her face showed the unpleasant shock at hearing Christian's talk of the vicar's betrothed.

"Gid… Mr. Bell that is. He is engaged?"

"Not anymore. Though I have no idea why. There was a lot of talk around the whole thing last year, but nobody seems to know what exactly went on. Claremont is an affluent and influential title, and nobody knows more than I that such things make one a target for gossips."

"Perhaps Elodie heard something about it."

"About what?"

Hope turned to see Elodie gliding toward them.

Hope rushed over to hug her sister, still marveling at the changes marriage to Christian had wrought in her, even now two years on.

Gone was the shy, demure lady who planted herself firmly in the background of any and all social interactions, and in her place was a confident, self-assured lady who smiled openly as she hugged her sister with equal exuberance.

"Your sisters met the Earl of Claremont and his brother. Apparently, he's to be the new vicar."

"Ah yes, Mama was just telling me about the earl's arrival. It seems the whole of Halton is swinging from the rafters about it. Seems you're not the only peer to cause something of a ruckus, my love," Elodie grinned up at her husband, who snagged a hand around her waist and pulled her toward him.

"But I am by far the most handsome, don't you think?" He winked before firmly planting a kiss on her lips.

"You're lucky Mama is not out here to witness your vulgar display," Hope scolded with mock severity.

"If you think that's vulgar…"

"Christian, why don't you go and stop Sophia from trying to drag herself up your horse?"

At Elodie's interruption of whatever scandalous thing Christian was doubtless about to say, the viscount's head snapped around to where Sophia was indeed attempting to launch herself onto Mercury's back.

"Sophia!" Christian's shout didn't even give the girl a moment's pause, and he rushed over, muttering under his breath as he went.

"So, why don't you tell me what you and Christian were gossiping about?" Elodie said gently, but she was watching Hope's face intently, her brown eyes boring into Hope's own.

"Your husband is worse than an old lady with his stories," Hope quipped as she took Elodie's arm and led her back to the house. "Sadly, his information was a little sparse. He tells me the vicar was engaged?"

"And this is interesting to you?"

Hope glanced sharply at Elodie, but her sister merely smiled serenely back.

"Only insofar as he is new to the neighborhood. I shouldn't like to commit some faux pas or other when speaking to him."

"Hmm. And we all know how conscious you are of never putting a foot wrong in a social situation."

Now Hope *knew* that Elle was teasing her. But before she could defend herself, Elodie continued and put her out of her misery.

"I've never met the vicar, though I am somewhat acquainted with his brother, the earl. But yes, I did hear that there was an engagement to a local woman that ended under strange circumstances. Nobody really knew what happened. The old earl passed away, and the current earl left the country abruptly. This was, oh, a year or so ago. Nobody has heard anything since. It was all a little mysterious, but you know the ton. It became old news as soon as the next *on dit* arrived."

Hope quietly absorbed everything Elodie told her. Elle had never been much of a gossip, and she wouldn't speculate about someone's life. She was far too kind for that, unfortunately.

And really, Hope shouldn't care. *Didn't* care. But…

"So, he's not engaged then?" She could have kicked herself for asking as soon as Elodie bit her lip in a gesture that Hope knew was to keep her from smiling.

"No, not to my knowledge in any case."

They walked in silence for a moment or two while Hope fought the urge to defend herself against Elodie's knowing smirk. It was the same as Cheska's and equally annoying. But she had a feeling that the more she argued, the more she'd convince her irritating sisters that she cared about the vicar. So, she kept her mouth shut until the silence grew unbearable.

Finally, she opened her mouth to tell Elodie in no uncertain terms that she didn't care a whit about whether Mr. Bell was single, engaged, married, or anything in between. But before she could even take a breath, Christian's shout rent the air, and they turned to see Sophia and Mercury jump a fence and tear off toward the fields with Christian racing after them both.

"It certainly won't be dull around here," Elodie laughed as her husband turned the air blue with his cursing.

"No, it certainly won't," Hope agreed, her own laugh sounding brittle in her ears.

She had a sneaking suspicion that being around the new reverend would be the furthest thing from dull. In fact, it would be quite the opposite.

Chapter Eight

"Oh, my dear Lady Brentford, how *wonderful* it is to have you home."

Hope couldn't help but roll her eyes at Mrs. Bell's exuberant greeting. She had practically shoved Hope out of the way to get to where Elodie stood with Christian, waiting to greet their hosts.

But rather than find it offensive, Hope merely gazed at Francesca, who'd been given the same treatment.

The vicar, at least, was more pleasant than his wife. As was Kit, or Lord Claremont, Hope supposed, who smiled and welcomed them as old friends.

A surreptitious glance told Hope there was no sign of Gideon. Surely the man wouldn't miss his own party? To ask after him would be abhorrent, especially after the teasing from both Cheska and Elle she'd endured on the way over here. Sophia had only refused to join in because she'd been too busy sulking about the taffeta on her ivory gown.

It wasn't especially fussy, they'd all assured her, but it was no use. As soon as she'd seen the pearls to accompany the gown, she'd refused to speak a single word to any of them.

"Is your brother not joining us this evening?" Cheska asked bluntly after the earl had bowed over both their hands. And Hope could have kissed her for her forthrightness.

"Ah, I–I am sure he will. At some point. He's not terribly fond of parties."

"But surely he must attend this one," Francesca pushed while Hope listened avidly to every word. "He's the reason we're all here, is he not?"

"Er…" The young lord looked flustered whilst he pulled at his cravat, and Hope couldn't help but think he was terribly meek to hold a title as lofty as the Earl of Claremont and the many responsibilities that surely came with it.

She had no idea just how far the arm of Claremont stretched since when she'd gone to research it, she'd found that the family's copy of *Debrett's* was missing. Questioning her sisters as to its whereabouts had resulted in an argument that had lasted until it was time to dress for the party, and so she was none the wiser.

Not that it mattered. Or had anything to do with her, come to that. She'd just been curious. And there was nothing wrong with a little curiosity.

Hope found herself chivvied along the receiving line before she could hear anything else about the whereabouts of Gideon, and so she reluctantly moved toward the large dining room where they would eat before dancing.

The Bells had made an effort with the decorations for to-night's party, and Hope took her time studying the arrangements of peonies and lilies in shades of white and pink as she moved around the room.

She knew everybody in attendance, and she smiled and batted her lashes. And she found herself vaguely wondering if she'd always found it so tedious here.

Perhaps it was just that after the size and noise of London, Halton seemed quieter and more unrefined than ever. Whatever it was, it left her feeling angsty and out of sorts, and suddenly the last thing she wanted was to sit at that table and either flirt shamelessly or fall asleep in her soup listening to the chatter of her mother and her cronies.

Hearing her mother's sycophantic tittering and Christian's long-suffering mumbling, spurred Hope into action. Her family would be here in seconds, and she'd be stuck. So, without looking left or right, she hurried as gracefully and nonchalantly as possible to the French doors, then slipped out into the blissfully quiet courtyard.

The sun was still shining overhead, and though it had cooled significantly, it was still warm enough that Hope didn't feel cold in her short-sleeved, daffodil-yellow dress. The color was so striking that Hope had only paired it with white gloves and a white ribbon in her hair. She'd been quite pleased with how she'd looked leaving the house, but now the dress felt like a beacon should anyone look for her. Even amongst the carefully tended flowerbeds of Mrs. Bell's modest garden, the gown stood out.

Cursing the satin material to perdition, she hurried out of sight of the doors. Thankfully, she knew this garden well having spent years running around it as a child while Mama took tea with the reverend's wife. And she knew that tucked away in a corner by the pond was the crumbling ruin of an old stone cottage. It had no doors, windows, or even a roof. But what it did have was the ability to hide someone who didn't wish to be seen from the house.

Hope knew this because she'd utilized it many, *many* times over the years along with her sisters. Excepting Elodie of course, who'd been happy to sit and take tea with Mrs. Bell since she'd been in short skirts.

Hitching the train of the gown up around her ankles, Hope made light work of hurrying down the garden path to the ruin. She couldn't hide forever, of course. Though it wouldn't be the first party she'd spent in the garden. Ordinarily, though, she at least had company. Cheska had almost always been with her on her dashes through Mrs. Bell's rose bushes. Still, if she could just take a moment alone, she would be well pleased.

Reaching the stone archway, Hope heaved a sigh of relief and stepped through it into blissful, peaceful silence.

"You don't strike me as the hiding type."

Hope screeched and spun around, a hand moving to press against her racing heart.

Standing behind her, grinning widely, was Mr. Bell.

"You scared the wits out of me," Hope complained.

"I can see that. You could wake the dead with your cater-wauling," he quipped. "Though they might forgive you once they see how delectable you look this evening."

Hope felt her jaw drop at the bold words, even as her heart stuttered. Oh, he was devilishly charming. As unlike a man of the cloth as any she'd ever encountered.

"Don't you think you should be inside, given that you're the guest of honor?" The words came out a touch more sharply than she'd intended. But she was more affected by seeing him than she liked, and his standing so close, the smell of his cologne, the breadth of his shoulders in his black superfine, the wicked glint in his dark eyes. It was overwhelming. And she wasn't used to being overwhelmed by men. Usually, it was quite the other way around, truth be told.

"Ah." Gideon stepped closer, and Hope had to steel herself not to move away. "Because the party is to welcome the new reverend."

"Er, yes," Hope answered hesitantly, confused by his odd phrasing. "Tell me, Mr. Bell, do you often refer to yourself in the third person?"

His grin was positively sinful.

"No," he answered softly. "Never."

Before she could question him further on yet another cryptic quip, he stepped closer still. This time, Hope did step away, only for her back to come into contact with the cool stone of the ramshackle cottage wall.

"So, why are you hiding?" he asked, that low, seductive voice shivering along her nerve endings.

"Who says I'm hiding?"

His mouth quirked in a way that set Hope's stomach flip-flopping alarmingly.

"Well, you ran down here as though the hounds of Hell were chasing you. And I can only assume that's because you didn't want anyone spotting you in your eye-catching gown. Unless ...”

His eyes, already the color of the most decadent chocolate, darkened suddenly as he frowned.

“Unless you're meeting someone here for an assignation?”

“I beg your pardon?” she asked, affronted, though she knew she shouldn't be. It wouldn't be the first time she'd snuck off to meet someone, after all. But she'd never allowed anyone to take more liberties than a kiss, and even at that, it was more a peck than anything else. In fact, only one man had ever kissed her fully on the lips. Eugene Jeffords, the apothecary's son, and it had been so grotesque that she'd shoved him away and spent the evening drinking gallons of bitter lemonade just to try to forget it.

“To my mind, there are only two reasons for a beautiful woman to be sneaking around the garden at a party. Either she's running *from* someone, or she's running *to* someone. So, which is it?”

“You are insufferably presumptuous, do you know that?”

She couldn't say why exactly she found his questions so irritating. Perhaps it was that the only man she *would* be interested in an assignation with was him. And he was surely far too moral to engage in such activities.

Vicars wanted ladies like Elodie. Not termagants like Hope.

“Not that it's any of your business, but I am not meeting anyone for anything. I just wanted some peace and quiet. Which is ruined now, thanks to you.”

Rather than look insulted, he looked fiercely amused. Perhaps even relieved.

“And might I remind you that you're out here, too. So, should I assume that *you* are out here for a secret tryst? Not exactly the lofty behavior of a man of the cloth, Mr. Bell.”

“My, my. What a temper you have. Does the idea of my meeting someone upset you so?”

Hope snorted in the most unladylike fashion. Sophia would be proud of such a sound.

“Why should I be upset? Surprised, perhaps. But upset? Hardly. Though I should imagine that such conduct will be intolerable to whichever poor woman ends up with you. Something to keep in mind when you…"

"Why does the idea of my being a reverend bother you so?" he interrupted rudely, as though he hadn't even heard a word she said.

"I–you–it doesn't bother me," she spluttered, well and truly up in the boughs without quite knowing why.

"Oh, I think it does," he answered smoothly. "And would you like to know what else I think?"

"Absolutely not," she barked, but again he ignored her.

"I think that you are as attracted to me as I am to you. I think that you feel the connection between us as much as I do. But for some reason, you are loathe to admit it. A vicar just isn't good enough, is that it? You're holding out for something better? Something loftier?"

Hope was so insulted by the scathing tone to his questions, by his assumptions, that she was some title-chaser, and truthfully, by her own body's reaction to his nearness, that she lashed out.

"That's exactly right," she spat, even though it absolutely *wasn't* right. "You think that I would take one look at that chiseled jaw and decide that it was worth lowering myself for? You presume to know me, to know what I'm thinking. Then you should know that someone like me would *never* deign to entertain a small-town vicar. Now, if you'll excuse me…"

His bark of humorless laughter stopped Hope in the act of stomping away, and she swung her head back to see anger flash in the dark depths of his eyes.

"I should have known," he said in a voice so filled with disdain that she winced. "You're all the same. Beautiful, far too aware of it, and far too willing to use it for your own machinations."

Hope's own anger was momentarily stalled by the bitterness in Gideon's words. He didn't know her well enough to have formed such an unflattering opinion of her character, so she knew that it must be something else, some other woman, perhaps his betrothed, to make him so hostile, so resentful. But it still hurt. And so, she lashed out some more.

"And why shouldn't I? If the whole world thinks my looks are the only worthy part of me, why shouldn't I use them to my advantage? Secure myself a title. Perhaps even an earl. Your brother is single, is he not?"

She wouldn't have thought it possible, but at her taunting words, Gideon's eyes grew darker still, and Hope swallowed nervously.

"Yes, he is. And decent and kind-hearted and good. Docile and unchallenging. All the things I am not. And all the things that you don't really want."

She opened her mouth to argue again. To tell him that he had no idea what she wanted.

But before she could get a word out, he pulled her firmly against him and pressed his lips against her own in a searing kiss.

Chapter Nine

G IDEON KNEW BETTER than to let his feelings get the better of
him. But damned if he didn't lose control every time he was
around the maddening, beautiful woman in his arms.

Never to the extent that he breached that final gap between
them. At least not until now.

But he'd taken leave of his senses apparently, for he was
allowing himself to be ruled by feelings alone. And the touch of
her mouth beneath his own was exquisite, as he'd known it
would be. With a muffled curse against her lips, the last of
Gideon's control snapped, and he reached up to clasp her face in
his hands, angling it so he could deepen their kiss.

Perhaps it was that need had finally won out over caution, or
that he'd seen red as jealousy clawed at him while she spoke of
another man, even his own brother, damn it, touching her like
this, holding her like this. Kissing her like this. He couldn't stand
the thought of it. Couldn't stand the thought of anyone being
right where he was now, being swept away in a tidal wave of
unadulterated lust.

He ran his tongue along her lip and used her gasp of surprise
to delve inside her mouth, delighting in her moan, exulting in her
arms snaking around his waist and pulling herself closer to him.

She was warm and pliant against him, the little sounds she
made in the back of her throat driving him wild, and when her
tongue darted out to dance with his own, Gideon couldn't

contain his desperate groan of desire.

He wanted her with a fierceness he'd never felt before. Not with Elaine. Not with any of the lovers or mistresses he'd taken over the years. It was a madness, a compulsion, a violent need that only grew with every second that he held her, every moment that he tasted her lips and inhaled the floral scent of her skin.

His hands moved as though of their own accord, one sweeping up to bury itself in the soft, smooth tendrils of her hair, the other to grasp the feminine flair of her hip, to pull her closer to the raging evidence of his desire.

This time, her gasp was tinged with a desperation that he knew matched his own. He could do it right now. Happily and irrevocably. He could lay her on the verdant grass beneath his feet and taste every inch of her, bury himself in her and take what he wanted. What *she* wanted, though, she might be too innocent to realize what her body was begging for.

It was that thought alone that pulled Gideon back from the brink of no return. Hope was the very embodiment of temptation, but she was innocent. And she deserved more than to have her virtue stolen by a man who was lying about his identity in a rundown cottage.

Reluctantly and with more strength than he knew he had, he pulled back from her, reaching out to steady her as she stumbled forward.

He watched, feeling a surge of masculine smugness as she opened dazed eyes and blinked rapidly. He'd done that. He'd put that blush on her cheeks, that glaze of lust in those eyes.

"That's one way to win an argument, I suppose."

Gideon blinked in shock at the irreverent tone, the outrageous quip.

He'd just kissed the wits out of her. The very least she could do was swoon a bit, he thought, feeling more than a little put out.

Here, he'd been having the very ground beneath him rock at the impact of their embrace. And she was making jokes.

Nobody and nothing had ever managed to put him quite so in

his place. To bruise his ego quite so well.

"I imagine that you hoped to shut me up by kissing me sense-less?" she continued, insultingly unperturbed by their kiss. "And you'll be happy to know that it worked. At least the shutting me up part. I think it would be better all-round if I returned to the rectory and behaved myself for the remainder of your party. I suggest you do the same."

Without another word or even a glance in his direction, she moved away from him and hurried up the garden, fixing her loosened curls as she went. He could only stare in bemusement as she tripped lightly up the steps, then took a deep breath, squared her shoulders, and glided inside.

Gideon didn't quite know what to do with himself. He cast his mind back, trying to remember a time that any woman of his acquaintance had been so singularly unimpressed with him. And came up blank.

Arrogant ass that he was, he'd never once questioned his skills in the seduction department. And he didn't much relish having to do so now.

And, of course, there was the small matter of that kiss only making him want Hope Templeworth even more than he had already. Which was a problem since he'd be in very public view of his aunt's guests soon enough.

Now that he knew she tasted as good as she looked, it would be a monumental task keeping himself in check. Which was why he was standing here like a goddamned green lad waiting for his body to get back under control before he went in there and clapped eyes on her again.

He thought back to their conversation. The one that had finally snapped his resolve. Her confirmation that she was just like every other lady of Quality; that she would sacrifice almost anything if it meant an advantageous match. That she would turn her back on desire or even love if it meant a title and wealth.

It shouldn't surprise him. It *didn't* surprise him. But he couldn't help the sting of disappointment any more than he could help his body from still wanting the little tearaway.

Heaving a sigh of his own, Gideon walked slowly back toward the house, feeling somewhat like he was walking to the gallows.

This misunderstanding of theirs had started out as a bit of fun. Let her think him a vicar. If she truly knew him at all, she would know that the very idea was laughable.

Now, he didn't want to tell her. Because if he saw that look in her eyes, the one that spoke to mercenary ambition, the one he'd seen in every damned ballroom across the continent, the one that had lit Elaine's eyes when she'd turned Kit's world asunder, well, he didn't think he could stomach it.

And yet, he knew he shouldn't care. What difference did it make to Gideon if some country chit acted in accordance with every other opportunistic debutante? He would leave this place soon. Leave Kit to the madcap town and all its residents. Would see little of Hope Templeworth. None of her, in fact, if she found herself a prize and moved away with him.

But as he walked inside his uncle's house and caught sight of her batting her lashes at Kit, he knew he cared. Very much cared. And that was a problem.

⇛⇚

HOPE'S LEGS WERE shaking so much that she was surprised nobody could see the movement under the folds of her gown.

She paid scant attention to whatever the perfectly nice but really rather boring Lord Claremont was saying because her entire focus was on his brother, who'd just walked into the room and sucked the air out of it.

Did nobody else notice? The size of him, the masculine presence surrounding him. It was most disconcerting. Intimidating even. It was why she'd had to work so hard in the garden to laugh off their embrace. To pretend it was nothing when inside of her, there'd been a cataclysmic shift the moment he'd touched her lips with his own.

And whilst she didn't have much scope for comparison, she could tell that he very much knew what he was doing.

Which begged the question, how had a vicar gotten so good at being wicked?

She watched surreptitiously as he wended his way through the small gathering until he ended up by Christian and Elodie's sides.

She watched as he bowed gallantly to Elodie, who smiled warmly in response.

And she watched as he reached out and shook Christian's hand. Shook his hand as though they were equals. As though Christian wasn't owed any subservience or honor as a viscount.

Strange. Though he'd alluded to knowing Christian and Elle, he surely didn't know them well enough to eschew the formalities of their titles?

Perhaps, because he was the son of an earl, and the brother of one now, he didn't feel the need to bow and scrape.

Realizing that she was spending far too much time staring and thinking about him, Hope turned away and cast an eye about the room.

Lord Claremont was engrossed in conversation with his aunt and uncle, along with Hope's mother and some of the other older ladies who ran Halton's charitable endeavors with iron fists.

Cheska was staring out a window and steadfastly ignoring any and all attempts at conversation, rolling her eyes at whomever was brave enough to approach.

Sophia was standing behind Mama, pulling at the neck of her gown and scowling as though she were in chains instead of lace.

She caught Hope's eye and rolled her own, the blue depths flashing with ire at being "frilled up and forced to act like a girl" to use her own words.

"Miss Templeworth. You are looking as lovely as ever."

Hope rolled her eyes at the familiar voice behind her.

Henry Fuller was a solicitor of some means. Handsome and pleasant enough but a veritable bore, truth be told. And he'd been pining after Hope since she'd been in long skirts.

She occasionally flirted and danced with him if she was ever bored or of a mind to humor him, but he knew that she wasn't at all interested. At least she hoped he knew. He *should* know. She had always treated their friendship with the same irreverence as she did everyone else of her acquaintance.

Pasting a smile onto her face, she turned to face the gentleman. He answered her smile with one of his own, his brown eyes, lighter than her own, raking over her with blatant appreciation.

It was a look she'd seen a thousand times before. A look that had no real effect on her anymore. In fact, there was only one man whose eyes had sent her nerves skittering in recent years when they gazed at her with such intensity. Such desire.

It was impossible to resist looking in his direction again, loathe as she was to do it. Hope's heart stuttered as her eyes connected with his own and she realized with a start that he'd been watching her from across the room. His scowling countenance darted to Henry, then back to Hope.

Her heart thudded painfully at his glowering stare. He looked furiously unhappy. He looked jealous!

That probably shouldn't please her, but Hope couldn't help the jolt of pleasure she felt at the idea of his being jealous. And remembering his arrogance in the garden, the assurance that he knew what she wanted, the way he'd turned her world upside down with that kiss, it awakened an imp of mischief inside of her.

And so, with an arrogant toss of her head, Hope turned back to Henry and beamed up at him, batting her lashes for good measure. She felt a tiny twinge of guilt when Henry's eyes widened slightly and his cheeks flushed. But he didn't seem unhappy about her attentions, so she figured there was no harm done.

Perhaps Mr. Bell needed to realize that he wasn't so irresistible. That there were other men who could hold her attention just as easily as he could. Even if it wasn't true, he didn't need to know that.

The Bells' ancient servant announced dinner, and Hope didn't hesitate to take Henry's arm, making sure to keep all her attention on him as they went through to the dining room.

Since Henry wasn't titled, he was her companion for dinner, and once he'd escorted her to her chair, she looked up the table to see if Gideon still seemed displeased. Her smug countenance turned to confusion. For Gideon was sitting directly across from Christian. And his brother, who *should* be seated higher up the table, seemed happily ensconced among the untitled members of their party.

In fact, looking around her, only she, Cheska, and Sophia seemed confused by the way everyone was seated, the way everyone seemed perfectly content to have an earl seated halfway down the table.

Glancing back up toward Gideon, she caught his grin, the lift of an eyebrow, and had a distinct impression that she was missing something.

But Henry was leaning forward asking her something, and so she dragged her eyes from the depthless darkness of his own and slipped on her most coquettish mask as she turned to the man by her side.

Chapter Ten

GIDEON'S MOOD HAD darkened so much by the time the ladies excused themselves to the drawing room that he wasn't surprised everyone gave him a wide berth.

Everyone but Christian Harrison that was.

Whilst the gentlemen sipped their port and enjoyed their cheroots, Gideon stared broodingly into his glass and tried to calm his temper.

He was beyond angry that Hope's father, useless oaf that he was, had sat there and allowed that country solicitor to salivate over his daughter. Even Christian, whom Gideon had shot daggers at all through dinner, had blithely ignored the man's carry on. He'd been only short of attacking her during the venison, damn it. And nobody had cared. Least of all Hope, who had maddeningly laughed and smiled and touched the bastard's arm so much, he was surprised she hadn't worn down the wool of his dinner jacket.

By the time the ladies were ready to retire, Gideon was ready to tear Fuller's offending arm off.

It was an overreaction. He knew that. Of course, he did. But there wasn't a damned thing he could do about it.

He scowled up at Brentford now, who'd stopped in front of him with an annoyingly knowing grin on his face.

"What could poor, harmless Mr. Fuller have done to earn your wrath, Claremont?" Christian asked with faux innocence.

"You've been staring at him as though you'd happily murder him where he sits all evening."

"I wasn't sure you knew of the man's existence, Brentford," he answered with a glare. "Considering you didn't seem to notice him when he was pawing at your sister-in-law during dinner."

The viscount's irritating smile only widened.

"I saw," he said while he sat uninvited in the chair beside Gideon's. "But it's hardly a rare occurrence around my sisters-in-law. Especially Hope. Sophia, thankfully, is still too young to attract much attention. Though that surely won't be long coming."

Brentford grimaced as he spoke, clearly anticipating an even bigger crowd of lovesick swains to contend with.

"And you're happy to just allow him to slobber over her like an animal? You and her father both?"

Christian's eyes darkened at the mention of Mr. Templeworth.

"You'll find that man gives not a damn about the lives of his daughters, Claremont," he snapped. "But regardless, what exactly was the problem? Hope enjoys the attention and, as I said, she is well used to it," he finished wryly, though his eyes were watchful as he took in Gideon's demeanor. "If I know anything about the Templeworth girls it's that they are very much able to take care of themselves and their own interests. If Hope didn't want the man's attention, she'd have done something about it."

Perhaps the other lord was trying to be reassuring, but he couldn't have said anything that would have darkened Gideon's mood further. So, Hope wanted the man salivating over her then. A far cry from the woman in the garden who'd spoken so callously about wanting to marry up.

"He is a mere solicitor," Gideon argued, desperately wanting Brentford to say that Hope wouldn't be caught dead with a solicitor, and then he'd misunderstood what he'd been witness to at dinner. "I wouldn't have thought such a man was lofty enough for the mercenary Miss Hope."

"Mercenary?" Brentford frowned. "I'm afraid you're very much mistaken. God knows, Hope can be accused of a lot of things but being avaricious certainly isn't one of them. I'd be more concerned with her falling desperately in love with a stable hand and eloping than setting her cap at a man just because of his title or deep pockets."

It was Gideon's turn to frown. Brentford's words were the complete opposite of what Hope had thrown at him in the garden before he'd kissed her within an inch of his life. Even now, the memory of that kiss had his body reacting in a way that was deuced uncomfortable in front of her brother-in-law.

The viscount's words were also absolutely sincere. He believed what he was saying, and Gideon didn't think that Hope would lie to her own family about wanting to marry up. Not when by all accounts it was her mother's fondest wish.

So why did she lie to him?

A snippet of her words flitted through his mind. *If the whole world thinks my looks are the only worthy part of me, why shouldn't I use them to my advantage?* Gideon felt a twinge of something unpleasant in his heart. Was it guilt? He'd let his jealousy cloud his judgment. His history make him cynical. And none of that was Hope's fault.

Had she lashed out, pretended to be scheming and greedy because of how he'd treated her? Was she really interested in this Fuller bloke? Or was she trying to prove some kind of point? And in the midst of all these maddening questions, one kept circling round and round—why did he give a damn?

"You should keep a closer eye on her," he groused when he realized that Brentford was still watching him, a knowing smirk on his face.

"Oh, I think you're doing enough of that for the both of us," the viscount quipped before standing up. "But just so there is no doubt, Claremont, I *am* watching."

It was a warning, no doubt about it. And Gideon couldn't blame the other man for issuing it. The entire *ton* had been made aware of the circumstances around Elaine's departure from their lives, and their father's subsequent death. No, that wasn't strictly true. The ton had no damned idea what had really happened, but it didn't stop them gossiping. The loose-tongued vipers never let a little thing like accuracy get in the way of their yapping.

But Brentford was bound to have heard something. Something enough to feel the need to warn Gideon away from Hope. Gideon wanted to defend himself. Wanted to assure the other man that there was no need for his protectiveness. That he'd already decided to stay the hell away from Hope Templeworth.

But then he thought of that kiss, those eyes, that smile, the wicked sense of humor and scant regard for propriety, and he kept his mouth shut.

Because if he were being honest with himself, he knew that Brentford was right. He had been keeping an eye on Hope. More than that. He'd wanted to kiss her senseless.

Yes, Brentford was right to warn him away. But Gideon had a suspicion that he wouldn't be able to stay away from Hope Templeworth. Even if he wanted to.

"I MUST SAY I'm quite surprised at you, Hope. I didn't think you'd be particularly interested in Henry Fuller, of all people."

Hope's snort was as unladylike as could be but thankfully Mama wasn't paying attention, and since her marriage to Christian, Elle wasn't such a stickler for rules and propriety.

They were all in the garden this morning, resting after last night's entertainment. Hope had managed to avoid Gideon by insisting that there be dancing and cards once the gentlemen had joined them in the drawing room.

And she'd made quite sure that she had a partner who was decidedly *not* him for every game of cards and for every single dance set. The only time she didn't dance, he'd been engaged with Francesca. And she hadn't been jealous. Not a bit. Not even when more than one person commented about how lovely Cheska's bright blonde curls looked against Gideon's dark coloring. How well they danced together.

Personally, Hope thought Francesca's shoulders had been a little slouched.

"You know full well that I am not interested in that man, Elle."

Elodie's smile was teasing.

"Of course, I know that," her sister answered. "The vicar then? Though I'm surprised at that, too."

Hope's stomach dropped to her kid boots as Elodie took a seat beside her on the wooden bench set against Mama's rose bushes.

"I–wh-what do you mean?" she stammered, her heart pounding.

Surely, she hadn't been obvious in her silly mooneyes for the man? She'd annoyed herself all evening by tracking his every movement, even while she'd pretended he didn't exist.

Surely her sister couldn't know that she'd tossed and turned all night, her sleep fitful, her dreams filled with dark-as-sin eyes and wicked smiles.

"You danced the night away with him, Hope! And though he is perfectly amiable, and it would be a suitable match, I didn't think your taste ran to someone so, well, so mild-mannered, frankly."

Hope could only stare at Elodie.

"And truth be told, I did wonder if perhaps there was something between you and the earl. I don't know him well, but anyone with a set of eyes could see how he watched you. Like he could devour you whole if given the chance. It was really quite something."

Her sister was stone mad. There was no other explanation for what she was saying.

"Elle, what *are* you talking about? I didn't dance a single dance with that great, big oaf. Nor would I want to," she lied, and hoped that her face didn't give her away.

Now it was Elodie's turn to look confused.

"Are you quite well?" Elle reached out and pressed a hand to Hope's forehead, which she promptly slapped away. Then hissed as Elodie slapped her arm in retaliation.

"Why are you beating each other senseless, and can I join in?"

Both Hope and Elodie turned as Francesca sat cross-legged on the grass in front of them, not caring a whit about her sky-blue skirts as she did so.

"We're not beating each other," Hope said. "But sadly, we need to have Elle committed to Bedlam. It seems she's quite lost her mind."

"I have not," Elodie interrupted. "But you might have done. How can you not remember dancing with the new reverend? I am full sure you're up to something, and you're probably involved, too." She turned to set an accusatory glare upon Cheska.

But Cheska looked equally confused by Elle's comments.

"Are you pregnant?" Francesca burst suddenly. "I've read that that can send you quite barmy. Especially in the first few weeks."

"Cheska!" Elodie's cheeks turned bright red, some of her old primness coming to the fore. "No, I am *not*. And if I was this would hardly be the way in which to discuss it," she sniffed. "Besides, I'm not *barmy*, as you so eloquently put it. I don't even know what you two are about. You seemed quite enamored of the new vicar, Hope. Even Christian noticed it. And he said the earl didn't seem at all happy about it. Though as I said, he watched you so closely, perhaps he was envious of his brother."

Hope opened her mouth to argue again with Elodie but then…

As though time slowed, every encounter, every conversation she'd had with Gideon sifted through her mind. She sat in stunned silence as she realized that she'd been wrong. That he'd deceived her.

His nasty accusation about her being a title hunter, a woman more interested in coin than love, that's why he'd been dishonest about who he really was. And he'd kissed her anyway. Why?

Because he's like every other man, a voice inside her spoke, *he took one look at you and didn't care about anything beyond your face.*

The disappointment and hurt at how little he must think of her were like a physical blow.

"The earl," she said now to Elodie, her teeth gritted. She wouldn't cry. She would refuse to be hurt. But she would allow herself to be angry. Furious. "He is the larger of the brothers? The one I danced with, he's the vicar?"

Elodie's frown of bafflement was answer enough. But she still spoke nonetheless. "Yes, of course," she said. "Just as I said. You danced with...Hope?"

Elle drew to a sudden halt as Hope jumped to her feet and stormed off to the bottom of the garden.

"Where are you going?" Elle's voice rang out, but Hope ignored her.

"Francesca! Get back here. What do you... Sophia! You can't leave in breeches, you must, oh for heaven's sake."

Hope only threw a look over her shoulder at Elodie's exasperated tone. Unsurprisingly, Cheska was hurrying after Hope, her face a picture of delighted anticipation. Elodie was scowling at Sophia, who must have heard the commotion from the stables and was now sprinting toward them, her breeches and boots caked in mud.

And it was so like old times that Hope almost smiled. Almost.

From the door of the conservatory, Christian appeared gaping at his wife.

"What is going on?" he shouted.

"Hope is hopping mad," Cheska called back. "I think she might murder the vicar! Or the earl, I suppose."

Christian, to his credit, didn't react beyond raising a brow. He had gotten well used to them by now, Hope supposed.

"Very well," he answered casually as though threats to the life of a man were positively mundane. Which they were, really, for the Templeworths. "Just don't leave me here alone for dinner."

"You're not helping, darling," Elodie called as she ran after Hope.

"I'll see you later, love. In time for dinner," was the only reply—and warning—the grinning viscount gave.

Chapter Eleven

"SHE WON'T ACTUALLY kill him, Elle. Honestly, you worry too much."

"Yes, it's a terrible bore. She'll probably only plant a facer on that handsome face in any case."

"It's not boring to stop your sister from being thrown into Newgate, Sophia."

"Ladies don't go to Newgate for punching earls," came their younger sister's tart retort. There was a slight pause before Sophia spoke again. "Do they?"

"I guess we're about to find out."

It was the first word Hope had spoken to any of them since she'd pieced together the clues Elodie had dropped in their garden. They'd arrived at the vicarage, and she was prepared to keep marching right up to the front door when Elodie appeared in front of her, blocking her way up the gravel path.

"Hope, I have no idea what is going on here, but you cannot…"

"He lied to me."

Elodie blinked in surprise. "Who did?" she asked.

"Gid… Mr. Bell, the *earl*," she finally spat. "He told me that he was the vicar. That his brother was the earl."

"But why would he do that?"

"That's an excellent question, Elodie," Hope's voice dripped with sarcasm. "One I intend to get the answer to right now."

She stepped purposefully around her sister, not waiting to see if they trailed after her but not one bit surprised that they did. She'd already banged on the door by the time they caught up to her.

The Bells' ancient housekeeper answered after only a moment, scowling until she spotted Elodie.

"My lady, how wonderful to see you again," she beamed. "Won't you come in? I'm afraid Mr. and Mrs. Bell aren't at home, but Lord Claremont and Mr. Bell would…"

"What luck. The earl is exactly who we're here to see."

Hope didn't give the housekeeper a chance to ignore her some more in favor of the revered Elodie as she stepped boldly into the modest foyer of the rectory and then stomped toward the drawing room, leaving Elodie to apologize profusely to the housekeeper who was now charging after Hope, Cheska, and Sophia, who'd skipped gaily after Hope.

There was a bit of a struggle at the closed door to the drawing room that Hope was a little ashamed of losing. Both she and Mrs. Tillman had grappled for the handle, and after an embarrassingly short battle, the older woman had gained purchase and shoved in front of the sisters to the unmistakable sound of Cheska's and Sophia's derisive snorts.

"Lady Brentford, my lord, Mr. Bell. And," there was no disguising the edge of distaste in the tone, "the Misses Templeworth."

The girls tripped over each other's skirts as they barreled into the room, not waiting to see if the gentlemen inside were willing to receive them. Only Elodie glided in like a lady.

Hope dimly registered the earl, no, Mr. Bell, the *actual* vicar, jump to his feet, his eyes on stalks. But most of her attention was on Gideon, Lord Claremont, as he rose slowly to stand.

The gentlemen bowed but, while Mr. Bell issued a greeting to all the ladies and requested a tea tray from Mrs. Tillman, Gideon spoke not a word, his eyes trained solely on Hope.

"What a pleasant surprise to see you all," Mr. Bell's voice

sounded a little weak as his eyes darted between Hope and Gideon. Neither of them acknowledged the remark. Neither of them moved. And Hope would be damned if she'd break first, so she just stood there, glaring, willing herself not to blink.

"Ah, I was so happy to properly meet you all at the party," Kit Bell rabbited on. Even Elodie was ignoring the man, as she, too, watched Hope and her nemesis. "Halton seems so lovely at this time of year and…"

"Mr. Bell," that was Francesca's voice, no-nonsense and firm. "With all due respect, I don't think any of us needs to chat about the weather. We all know why we're here, so why don't we watch silently to see how things unfold, lest we miss something?"

It was as outrageous a statement as Cheska had ever made, and Hope dimly heard Elodie's sigh of exasperation. But Francesca was honest to a fault if nothing else. Her sisters were here to see her confrontation with the man who'd lied to her. Perhaps Elodie was here to ensure no blood was spilled, but she was the only one.

"I'm afraid you have us at a disadvantage, Miss Temple-worth," Gideon addressed Cheska's bold statement, whilst his brother stammered and stuttered in shock. But he kept his eyes on Hope. "I have no idea why you're here, though I agree with Kit. It is a pleasant surprise."

Hope tried not to shiver at the invitation in his tone, his voice dropping to an almost growl. Hell would freeze over before she'd let him see that he had any kind of effect on her. "But given that your sister looks like she'd happily have my head, I'm guessing that I'm in some sort of trouble?"

His cavalier attitude only riled Hope further.

"Of course not," her voice was saccharine, and Hope gritted her teeth as Sophia whispered, "oh he's in *big* trouble."

"Surely your behavior is above reproach." Hope paused before continuing. "*My lord.*"

"Ah."

That was it. He made no move to speak further. No move to

defend himself or apologize or anything. He just stood. And stared.

"Ah?"

"*Ah?*" she repeated incredulously. "That's all you have to say? Ah?"

She waited again for him to apologize, to be ashamed, perhaps even throw in a little groveling.

But there was only that slow, wicked grin. And her damnable reaction to it, even now, even knowing that he'd deceived her, thought her so mercenary that he had hidden his wealth and title from her. She wanted to hate him. But she couldn't. And she was in a world of that big trouble Sophia had whispered about.

⇶✦⇷

GIDEON KNEW HE shouldn't see Hope's anger as some sort of aphrodisiac, but damn if his body didn't stir as her voice dipped dangerously low.

He'd spent last night getting well and truly foxed, his jealousy and anger growing with every smile Hope sent someone else's way, every turn around the small dance space that wasn't in his arms.

In fact, the only thing that had stopped him from dragging Kit by the scruff away from the little hoyden was one small, fledgling iota of common sense still left in his drunken stupor. But he'd kept a close eye. On her, on his brother, on that drooling Fuller person. While he'd danced with the sister, her blue eyes so much sharper and icier than Hope's, as she watched him shrewdly knowing, he'd kept watching.

He was a damned fool. In ways that he had never been before. Not with Elaine. Not with anyone.

And even knowing that, standing here facing her anger, her sisters' delighted nosiness, he still wanted her. Though who wouldn't, he wondered, when she was so utterly delectable. She looked like a breath of fresh, summer air in her soft pink skirts, her caramel curls tumbling unchecked down her slender back.

He didn't know a single woman of Quality who would stomp around the countryside so uncaring about how she would appear. And he was utterly enchanted by it, even if he didn't want to be.

"If I recall correctly, it was you who decided introductions were unnecessary that day at the lake."

"What day at the lake?"

Gideon snapped his eyes to Lady Brentford, who looked annoyed yet not entirely surprised to hear of a hitherto unknown meeting at the lake. He looked back to Hope, wondering if she'd be upset at the disapproving tone in her sister's voice. But as he suspected, she was marvelously unbothered.

"I met him when I was swimming in a lake," she responded without taking her eyes from Gideon. "And yes, I was practically naked. And no, I don't care if it is deemed scandalous or unlady-like, so don't bother with a sermon."

There was utter silence for a few seconds before the viscountess sighed. "I wasn't going to give you a sermon," she said softly, but even Gideon didn't believe her.

"Um," Kit's voice sounded, drawing everyone's attention, and Gideon's watched with a sort of savage amusement as his brother's cheeks turned scarlet and sweat beaded on his brow. "I cannot claim to understand fully what is happening here, b-but I'm not sure that I should be privy to-to such talk. P-perhaps I should…"

"Perhaps you should explain why you went along with it, Mr. Bell. Not very godly of you."

Kit's reddened cheeks paled under Miss Francesca's icy tone, and Gideon felt a tiny twinge of guilt that his poor, naïve brother was in the clutches of the angry Templeworths.

"Kit knew nothing of it, save for that day at the inn. And I asked him to stay quiet about that."

"What day at the inn?" the viscountess once again spoke. "What am I missing?"

"Loads," Sophia Templeworth added most unhelpfully. "But hush for now in case we miss anything else."

"Yes, I do believe the earl, the real one, was about to explain why he asked a man of the cloth to lie to Hope's face. Not a great start to a flourishing career in Halton, if you don't mind me saying so, Mr. Bell."

Francesca's tone was freezing, and she raised a brow at poor Kit, who gulped so loudly that Gideon heard it from across the room.

"My apologies to you, Miss Hope. But Gideon, that is to say, Lord Claremont had explained that there was a misunderstanding and, and…"

A knock sounded on the door interrupting poor Kit's bumbling in the face of four sets of narrowed eyes.

The knock had heralded the arrival of a tea tray, and Gideon watched in a sort of faint amusement as Kit's skin turned bone white, relief stamped on his face.

"Perhaps, Miss Templeworth, you and I could take a walk in the garden to discuss this more privately."

He'd let his voice drop on purpose, putting a world of innuendo in that tone, and he knew she knew it, too, from the flare of emotion in her brown eyes. Not entirely anger, but something far more pleasant than that. Maybe she couldn't help the attraction any more than he could.

"I hardly think leaving you two alone would be prudent," the viscountess sniffed, her face becoming a mask of ladylike propriety.

In response, her sisters snorted derisively in perfect unison. Clearly a lot less concerned with the strictures of polite society.

"Go ahead Hope, go and listen to his excuses. But be sure to tell us everything."

"Hope, do not go anywhere."

Gideon watched the blonde and brunette behind Hope glare at each other. They were akin to an angel and a devil on her shoulder, yet the blue-eyed blonde was certainly the devilish one.

No doubt about it.

"I'd take a seat if I were you, Mr. Bell. This sort of thing can go on for hours." This from the youngest who'd planted herself on the chaise without invitation and was already filling a plate with the delicate cakes and biscuits Cook had provided.

"Days even, once Hope gets involved," she said, her voice muffled now around a bite of what looked to be apple pie.

They were stark, staring mad, every one of them. He'd heard of flouting propriety, but the Templeworths were something else. A volcano wrapped in a hurricane covered by a tsunami. And Gideon wasn't sure he'd survive it.

"Sophia, do not speak with your mouth full. You... Hope!" The viscountess shook her head.

Apparently, Hope had only been waiting for one of the other little hoydens to do something wrong before she made a break for it, and he turned to follow her, feeling like a naughty schoolboy as they raced into the garden.

Hope darted onto the path that led to the ramshackle cottage where they'd kissed, and Gideon's heart hammered in response, which was, of course, ridiculous.

He didn't know if Hope suddenly realized it, too, because she suddenly changed direction, walking, no stomping instead to a small, white gazebo at the other side of the garden. And he followed, unable to resist admiring the sway of her hips as she went. He followed all the way up the wooden steps, into the center of the tiny building, and drew to a stop, mere inches from where she spun around to glower at him.

"I would have told you who I was," he started before she could shout at him again. "But it was nice. Knowing that you didn't see my title. My wealth. Didn't know enough about me to want me for those things."

If he'd been hoping that his words would cool her ire, he was sorely mistaken, for he saw the exact moment that her temper flared even hotter, sure that if he looked closely, he might see literal flames in her eyes.

"So, I didn't know anything about you, but you apparently knew enough about me to assume I *would* want your money and titles?" she asked, her voice quiet and all the more terrifying for it.

"No, I just…"

He wasn't sure how to explain it all. Elaine, Kit, his father. All of it. But the longer they stood there, the more guilt at his duplicity gnawed at him. He'd thought it a harmless joke. Had been amused by the idea of someone thinking he, of all people, was a vicar. But that was real hurt flashing beneath the temper in her eyes. And though it was crazy, though they barely knew each other, he found that he could think of little worse than hurting the woman glaring at him right now.

"You just what? You just thought to make a fool of me for your own entertainment? You just thought to throw accusations of avariciousness at me, while kissing me and using me for your own selfish gains?"

Well, when she put it like that it sounded even bloody worse!

"I …"

"No, don't trouble yourself, my lord," she continued before he could defend himself. Her voice dripping with saccharine venom, his title never sounding more like an insult. "Because luckily for you, I don't want your titles. I don't want your money. I don't want *you* at all."

And before he could reach out, or utter a single word, she flew pass him and marched right back out of the gazebo, then the garden, and, he assumed, the house.

Gideon just stood there. Feeling like the blackguard that he suspected he was.

Chapter Twelve

S HE WAS BEAUTIFUL, *in that sultry way that implied she would know what she was doing in the bedchamber. And that happened to be the exact type of beauty that suited Gideon just fine.*

He smirked as she dropped her eyes from his own, not buying the coquettish act for a moment. In fact, he would bet everything that he'd won at the vingt-et-un *table this evening that she'd be looking right back at him in five...four...three...two...*

He allowed his grin to widen as sure enough, her blue eyes once more swept to his own in blatant invitation.

Gideon felt a smug satisfaction even as his cock twitched in anticipation of being buried in her. Weeks on the road without female companionship would do that to a man, he supposed.

He had no idea who this raven-haired beauty was, but he sure as hell wanted to find out. He finished his round of cards, casually dropping another winning hand onto the table before excusing himself and sauntering over to her.

Manners would dictate that he await an introduction and not speak freely to a lady he'd never met. But thankfully, this wasn't exactly the type of establishment that lent itself to polite Society manners. There'd be plenty of time for that nonsense when he returned to the family fold tomorrow. When he visited his father's Mayfair townhouse having spent the first half of the Season overseeing repairs at one of their country estates.

He'd refused to stay in the London house with his father and Kit, choosing instead to stay in rooms at his club and thoroughly enjoy his bachelorhood.

In fact, he hadn't even informed the earl or Kit of his arrival in Town, choosing to keep a low profile for a spell whilst he indulged in the proclivities that neither of them exactly approved of. And since Kit's letters had been full of flowery prose about his sweet, innocent Miss Samson, Gideon figured he'd be even less approving.

"You are far too beautiful to be spending the evening alone." He grinned down at the lady who was batting her lashes at him.

For a wild moment, Gideon felt vaguely disgusted. At himself and at whomever this woman was. This game they played. This dance that led to tupping and nothing else. It felt distasteful. The thought surprised him. He had no idea when he'd begun to think in this way. Perhaps Kit was rubbing off on him.

"I am not alone now, am I, my lord?" She smiled seductively.

"You know who I am?" He wasn't surprised, really. The Claremont dynasty was widely known and being the viscount, the heir, meant his name got around.

"I've only just learned," she answered, and as she spoke, Gideon saw that beneath the sultry heat of her gaze, there was a coldness that he hadn't spotted from across the crowded gaming hall. She put him in mind of a viper sizing up her prey. "I admit, I was surprised to see just how handsome you are. I didn't think you would be."

Her statement was cryptic enough to give Gideon pause. Clearly, she'd been speaking to someone about him. In quite a bit of detail, apparently. Yet, if she was just another Society miss hell-bent on a title, wouldn't she be frequenting the gilded ballrooms of the beau monde? Not slumming it in a gaming hell in the Seven Dials. This was no place for a lady. Not one of Quality, in any case. Yet, though she was well-spoken, she didn't have those cultivated tones of the ton ladies. Perhaps a wealthy merchant's daughter or a gentleman farmer's, then.

"A pleasant surprise I hope," he quipped, but his heart wasn't in it. The feeling of discomfort arose again. "Well, I'm sure that you want to get back to whomever you came with this evening." He made to step away, but her hand on his arm stopped him.

"I came alone," she purred. "But I'm hoping I won't leave that way."

And base bastard that he was, Gideon buried all his misgivings. She was beautiful and willing, and why the hell not? So, he answered her blatant invitation with his most charming smile, then took her home to bed her.

"THAT WAS QUITE the visit."

Kit's wry tone pulled Gideon from memories that he hadn't allowed to surface since the tragedy last year. Why he was allowing himself to stew on it now, he had no idea. Perhaps because he knew that his experience with Elaine and with Kit and with their foolish, deceased father had colored his view of Hope Templeworth to the point that the accusations she'd flung at him earlier.

"Indeed," he answered as steadily as he could. "But then, I suspect that every encounter with the Templeworth girls is quite the visit," he added. "Especially Hope."

"Ah yes, the beautiful Hope. She is astonishingly pretty," Kit answered, and Gideon had to forcibly shove aside a ridiculous surge of possessiveness at Kit's words. They were true in any case, were they not? Anyone could see how beautiful she was. "But then you already know that," his brother continued, and Gideon's eyes snapped up to see Kit grinning slyly at him.

"What do you mean?" he asked carefully.

"I mean that there is quite clearly *something* between you and the lady, Gideon. The air fairly crackles around you both. And I've never seen you so overset in the company of a woman. If I didn't know better, I'd say that you were becoming quite smitten with the girl."

Gideon had to make a concerted effort to school his features into a mask of indifference.

"What romantic tosh," he laughed, albeit a little hoarsely. "You know that one woman is pretty much the same as another to me."

But even as he said the words, they rang hollow to him, setting his heart fluttering in panic.

"Hmm. That *has* been true," Kit said thoughtfully. His brown eyes, lighter than his own almost black, squinted slightly. "Or at least it has been before. I don't know, but there just seems to be something about the girl. Or about how you are with the girl at least."

Gideon jumped up from where he'd been sitting on an over-stuffed armchair, a decanter of brandy at his side.

"Turning your mind to matchmaking little brother?" he asked, desperately striving to keep his tone light, even arrogant. "Shouldn't you be looking toward your own relationships first? After all, a good vicar must surely set an example for his flock. Settle down with a nice lady. Raise a brood of God-fearing children and all that?"

"Why yes, I suppose I should," Kit parried. There was a pause before he continued, his tone carefully neutral. "There's no denying that the Templeworths would be an excellent family to marry into. Connected to Brentford. Uncommonly attractive. Yes, perhaps I *should* be concentrating on myself."

Gideon quirked a brow.

"No offense, Kit. But Francesca Templeworth would eat you alive," he warned. He couldn't even imagine it; Kit trying to survive the force of nature that the blonde, blue-eyed Francesca Templeworth was. He couldn't think of any man who could do so, truth be told.

In actual fact, Kit's face paled dramatically at the mere suggestion.

"Er, no, no I do not think we should suit," he gulped. "She is rather intimidating, isn't she?"

Gideon forgot his maudlin thoughts in the face of Kit's utter terror. And the smile he offered his brother this time was genuine.

"Don't worry, Kit. I won't let her near you. But you can't mean the girl," he added sternly. "She is but a child."

Kit looked suitably horrified, which put Gideon at ease immediately.

"Of course not, what do you take me for?"

But Gideon's relief was short-lived. For there was only one available Templeworth left.

"You can't mean…"

Gideon couldn't even finish the sentence. His stomach roiled. They couldn't be back here. Not again. Not after what had happened between them before.

"Hope," Kit answered gently, and Gideon recoiled from the sudden pity in his younger brother's face. "As a matter of fact, I did mean her. But not seriously. I just thought to get your reaction. And I think I have my answer as to your true feelings. Even if you don't yet realize it."

"It's not what you think," Gideon argued, but there was no bite in it. He heard it, and Kit surely did.

"I don't think anything." Kit shrugged. "Don't get angry, Gideon."

Gideon braced himself, knowing by Kit's sudden seriousness that he wouldn't like what was coming.

"Not every woman is Elaine," his brother said. There was no bitterness in his voice, no resentment in his open face. Though there should have been. If he wasn't so damnably *good*, there would have been. And maybe the Gideon wouldn't feel so guilty. Even now.

"I know that" he rasped.

"Do you?"

Gideon couldn't abide the gentle understanding in Kit's voice.

"You let the past control you, Gideon. You didn't know what Elaine was about, neither of us did. I didn't blame you then, and I don't blame you now. Yet you continue to blame yourself, and it's affecting you. Perhaps in a way that you don't even under-stand the detriment of yet."

Gideon wasn't in the mood for cryptic remarks any more than he was in the mood for a sermon from his vicar brother. And whilst Kit might have been able to move on, to forgive and forget, not just his own treachery, accidental though it might have been, but their father's and even Elaine's, Gideon could not. Would not.

The only innocent party in the whole mess was Kit. None of them deserved his forgiveness. The bastard who'd sired them certainly didn't. And the woman who'd cuckolded Kit with both his brother *and* his own bloody father? She deserved it even less so. The thought still turned Gideon's stomach, even after all this time. He still couldn't face up to it, could barely stand to look at himself in the mirror some days.

And as that thought sank into his mind like a stone, so, too, did the knowledge that Kit was right. His self-loathing about how he'd allowed Elaine to use him in her scheming, his mistrust of beautiful women, the desire to get away that had driven him to this insane town, all came tumbling into place.

Hope had been right. He'd kept his identity from her because he didn't trust her not to want his title, money, and good name. Not at first. At first, it had just been a bit of fun with a beautiful stranger at a lake. But the more he'd seen her, and then that kiss, well, at some point it started to just be plain deceit. And though he should know better than to think any of those things would matter to her, it hadn't stopped him from being a complete blackguard to her.

He owed her an apology. A real, sincere one. And possibly an explanation if he hoped to keep her in his life. Though it was far too soon to put any sort of effort into staying around her, of course. Gideon knew that. Knew that in only weeks he would be moving home. Would be going back to his quiet, bachelor life. The life he wanted...wasn't it?

His circuitous thoughts weren't bringing him any relief. Nor was the guilt still clawing at him, obviously.

Kit's sigh caught Gideon's attention, and he looked up to see not only disappointment but worse, pity in his younger brother's stare.

"I'll fix it," he told Kit who nodded his satisfaction before slipping from the room.

Yes, he'd fix it. But damned if he knew how.

Chapter Thirteen

HOPE DESCENDED THE stairs of the manor house, and her family gaped at her. Mama looked proud, and Christian was scowling. Elodie looked suspicious. Francesca grinned wickedly. And Sophia, who was seeing them all off, still in her breeches and stuffing her face with an apple tart, ran an eye over Hope then snorted. "You're only going into Halton, Hope. Do you think the Regent is going to turn up or something?"

"I don't know what you mean," Hope sniffed.

"I mean it's the Assembly Rooms. Not Almack's or St. James's. Why are you dressed for a coronation?"

"What? I can't wear a nice dress? Not all of us wish to dress like boys, you know."

"Hmm. And not all of us are so concerned with that lying scoundrel Claremont that we feel the need to dress like royalty for a country dance."

Hope darted out a hand and snatched Sophia's tart from her, holding it above her head where her little sister couldn't reach and demanding an apology. The noise of the ensuing argument had been louder than usual, Hope conceded later as they traveled to the dance. And the tousle that had left Sophia's apple tart squished beyond repair and Hope's hair disheveled and falling out of its painstakingly pinned style had taken an age to sort out.

There'd only been time to replace Hope's spoiled gloves and pin a few tendrils of her hair back from her face, leaving the rest to tumble in waves down her back. Cheska had laughed herself silly. Elodie had scolded them all, but there was no real bite to it. And poor Christian had been left to deal with Mama.

But they were here now, and Hope could admit to herself if nobody else, that Sophia had been right. Her champagne-colored satin gown was more suited to the gilded ballroom of an elaborate London event, and not the modest rooms of Halton's Assembly Hall. The neckline plunged enough that she knew it would be considered daring, perhaps even scandalous by Halton standards. The dress was simply cut and decorated only with seed pearls, but it somehow managed to look extravagant against her curls, the light color highlighting her brown eyes.

Ivory slippers and gloves, a satin ivory fan, and pearls at her ears and throat completed the look.

"Hope, do try to behave yourself tonight, won't you?"

Hope looked up from straightening a glove to see Christian frowning at her from outside the carriage, his hand extended to help her alight.

"Probably not, no." She grinned unrepentantly.

"Not even for my sake?" he asked, his blue eyes imploring.

"Especially not for your sake," she laughed.

"You wound me," Christian said dramatically before releasing her hand. "Just—warn me, please. If any of you is planning to make a break for it."

The reference to the time Elodie had run away made Hope laugh harder. She'd been the one to take pity on Christian and help him get to Elle in the end.

As if her brother-in-law was also remembering that, remembering how close he'd come to losing his viscountess, he reached out and pulled Elodie toward him, tucking her into his side. Hope couldn't help but sigh as Elle looked up at Christian, her eyes filled with tenderness, even as confusion was obvious on her face.

"Are you well?" she asked, and Christian bent his head to press a kiss against her brow.

"Never better," he answered softly, ignoring their mother's

hiss of disapproval. He'd never cared about Mama's opinion. Never worried about the fact that most members of the *ton* barely acknowledged each other's existence in public. He had always kissed, touched, and flirted outrageously with his wife no matter the place, no matter the occasion. "Just remembering to keep you close. Being back here, it reminds me of certain things."

Elodie rolled her eyes, even as she laughed.

"That was two years ago, darling."

"Call it nostalgia," Christian answered dryly. "Don't you remember that this is where you accosted me for the first time?"

"I think you'll find that this is where you wouldn't mind your own business when I had to chase a thoroughly foxed Francesca out here."

"Ah yes, that does sound more like it." Christian winked as he began to escort them inside the building. "Remind me to thank her later." Then his tone dropped as Hope hurried ahead of them both. But she still heard him as she stepped inside the foyer of the rooms. "And show *you* just what I'm thankful for."

⋙✕⋘

"YOU KNOW, I never realized just how *fascinating* the anatomy of a moth truly was, Lord Winston. Please, do go on."

Hope smiled prettily as she lied through her teeth at the young baron whilst inwardly, she wondered if one of the ivory bones of her silk fan would be thin enough to burst her eardrums so she wouldn't have to listen to any more of his incessant chatter.

She'd never given much thought to the lifespan or even the existence of moths before. Now she hated them viscerally. Which seemed rather unfair since they'd never personally offended her.

But she reminded herself, listening to the boring baron waffle on about his odd obsession was a small price to pay if the result was avoiding Gideon whose eyes, even now, bored into her from across the room.

For three days he'd been calling on her. And for three days she'd refused to see him. Tonight's ball in the Assembly Rooms, a sort of *goodbye* for Mr. and Mrs. Bell was unavoidable according to Elle, and so she'd come.

From the moment she'd stepped into the rooms, there he'd been. His dark gaze focused so wholly on her that she felt as though he were peering into her very soul. The heat of that gaze alone had her cheeks burning, and she'd swiftly looked away before anyone noticed.

And so it had been for above two hours now. A never-ending game of cat and mouse. Every time Hope sensed Gideon's presence, she found another group to talk to. She filled her dance card within seconds of entering, saying yes to gentlemen that she would usually refuse. And when all of that failed, she shamelessly hid in the ladies' retiring room.

But now she was stuck here with Lord Winston and his flying bugs, ignoring Gideon's stare, and feeling her eyes glaze over. The next set was a quadrille. A dance she'd left open on her card because Lord Winston was as bad a dancer as he was a conversationalist, and she really didn't want to get these slippers ruined. So in lieu of accepting his offer, and because she didn't want to be left standing on the edge of the dancers with the earl watching her every move, she'd feigned an interest in his hobby.

And she would regret that decision every day for the rest of her life.

"You know," Lord Winston's tone suddenly dropped an octave, and he stepped closer, alarmingly close, in fact. "If I'd known you had a mind for science, I would have made my interest in you known before now, Miss Templeworth."

Hope leaned back enough that she almost fell over.

"I beg your pardon?" she gasped.

"Well, as beautiful as you are, nobody truly wants a stupid wife. But now that I know you share my passions," his smile turned positively lecherous, his spectacles sliding down his freckled nose, "Well, I'm sure there's plenty more we could…"

"Lord Winston." Hope took a very deliberate step back. "I think there must be a misunderstanding."

She'd known the man since she'd been in leading strings. And he'd never been foolish enough to find her flirtations anything more than just that. So, to have him stand before her now in a crowded ballroom, and practically declare himself, well, it was ridiculous, and she wasn't in the mood to humor it.

"No misunderstanding, Miss Hope. After all, you've come back from London single year after year. You've never shown an interest in any of the dandies and fops around here. I often wondered why, thinking you as foolish and vacuous as they."

Hope could only gasp at the man's audacity, the insult flowing from his lips even while he continued to leer at her.

"But now that I know you have brains as well as beauty? Well…" He laughed and moved closer still. Now only inches separated them. He was close enough to kiss her, she realized with no small measure of disgust. "It seems worth it to throw my hat in the ring, in a manner of speaking."

Hope's temper flared at Lord Winston's disdainful words. Close enough to kiss also meant close enough to be punched on the nose. Something she very much wanted to do right now.

"Sir Winston, let me be clear. I have no interest in …"

Hope's words were cut off by Lord Winston pressing a fleshy finger against her lips.

"Sir Mwmpstmn!"

She couldn't even form a coherent word around the digit.

"Shh." He smiled beatifically at her given that she had a couple of inches on him. "You don't need to speak, my dear. I shall speak to your father and…"

Right. That was enough of that.

Hope smacked Lord Winston's hand away from her mouth, resisting the urge to spit as she did so.

"My dear."

"I'm not your bloody dear," she gasped, so fed up she was

practically breathing fire.

"There you are. I believe the next is mine, Miss Temple-worth?"

Hope and Lord Winston's ridiculous argument drew to a sudden halt as another voice sounded behind Hope.

Of course, she thought exasperatedly. *Of course, he's here.*

Inhaling through her nose in an attempt to calm her scorching temper, Hope spun around to face Gideon, who was gazing smugly down at her as though he'd rescued her like some sort of damsel in distress.

"Then you believe wrong," she bit in her iciest tone. "Now, if you'll both excuse me, I have no intention of speaking to either of you for the rest of the evening."

She made to step around Gideon, completely ignoring the bullheaded baron behind her. But to her intense annoyance, he merely reached out a hand and clasped her gently but firmly around her upper arm.

His touch felt like a brand as his fingers closed around the exposed skin between her glove and the short sleeve of her gown, and Hope had to swallow a sudden lump in her throat.

"Let me go," she demanded through gritted teeth.

Gideon's smile was positively wicked. "No, I don't think I will," he said casually as though he weren't accosting her in a crowded ballroom. "We can dance, or we can take a walk outside. But I'm not letting you go until you talk to me."

"I don't know who you think you are, but…"

"I'm a man who has hurt you and is grievously sorry," he said softly, stopping her tirade in its tracks. "So please, do me the honor of allowing me to apologize." The sincerity in his face melted into something far more mischievous. "Or should I wait until you and Lord Winston have finalized things?"

Her answering scowl clearly didn't intimidate him, for he merely laughed as he dropped her arm but held out a hand.

"Miss Templeworth, may I?"

"No, you may not," she snapped over her shoulder, not even

allowing Lord Winston to finish whatever tripe he was about to come out with. But though she addressed the sniveling baron, she kept her eyes on the earl.

"What's it to be, Hope?" he asked, his large hand still extended.

She wanted to tell him to go to Hades and march out of the room. But he'd follow.

She wanted to ignore the hand he offered and find some other willing man to dance with. But he'd wait.

So, quickly deciding that dancing was the lesser of two evils because at least they wouldn't be alone, she took his hand and dragged him toward the formation already lining up, the modest orchestra plucking the opening strings of the quadrille.

And as she faced him, glaring in the face of his smug smile, ignoring the admiring looks from the gentlemen around her, she began to wonder if she'd met her match.

Chapter Fourteen

S HE WAS A vision. A goddess. An enchantress under whose spell every red-blooded man in the room was falling. And Gideon was no exception.

He'd tried for days to speak to her. Growing ever more desperate to do so. She'd ignored every attempt. But this evening, he didn't think his heart had yet recovered from that first glimpse of her.

And he knew the second her beautiful eyes landed on him, then swiftly moved away, he knew that she would continue to ignore him if he allowed it. And that she'd probably slap his face if he approached her at the wrong time. So, he'd waited. Watched. Half amused, half angered by the stream of men desperate to get her attention. One smile from her had most of them nearly wilting to the floor. But did none of them notice that it wasn't sincere? It was the smile of a coquette, beautiful but empty. Not her true smile, the one laced with fire and mischief.

The one that made Gideon's gut clench. With desire, yes. But something more, too. Something unfamiliar and tender, and all the more terrifying for it.

He'd been happy to keep his distance. One eye on Hope, the other on her many, *many* suitors, until that odious little weasel, some baron or other, began to crowd her. Having no doubt that she was quite capable of handling herself, Gideon still felt his temper rise as he watched the odious little rat practically plaster himself to Hope's body.

Before he'd even known what he was about, Gideon found his feet moving toward them. From the corner of his eye, he spotted the other sister, Francesca, as she lifted her head and scowled across the room. Even from here, Gideon saw her eyes flash venomously at the baron. And if the other man hadn't been pawing at Hope, he might have actually felt sorry for him.

As it was, it appeared to be a race between them to see who'd get to Hope first. Gideon, who was moving smoothly through the ensemble trying not to draw too much attention, or Francesca Templeworth who threw back the full glass of champagne she'd been holding, then slammed it on the refreshment table and stomped across the room like a general going into battle.

Gideon didn't know if it was a good thing that he'd gotten there first or not. A part of him was quite simply terrified of the diminutive, icy-eyed blonde. But to his surprise, she'd stalled on the peripheral of Hope's sight, eyed him closely for a few, interminable seconds, and then given him what he could only assume was a nod of acceptance. Or permission, at least, to be the one to step in.

So now here he stood, nervous as a schoolboy, while Hope determinedly looked anywhere but at him. And he wanted those eyes upon him quite desperately, Gideon realized with no small amount of surprise. Even if they were glaring at him.

The dance began, and Gideon couldn't hold back his grin as Hope barely curtsied before sticking her nose back up in the air and ignoring him once again.

The steps took them close enough for him to smell that fresh, summer meadow scent that seemed to linger long after she'd left a room. A scent that he'd been dreaming of like a madman.

"You look stunning," he said softly, so only she could hear.

"I know," she bit back but without conceit, and Gideon chuckled softly.

They clasped hands, and he had to work to contain a shudder of pleasure at even that merest of touches.

"Some people might accuse you of vanity, Miss Temple-worth, if you don't simper and giggle when someone pays you a compliment."

"I'd have to care about people's opinions for that to matter to me, Lord Claremont. And I do not. Especially yours."

Damn, but she was vicious. She could flay a man alive with that tongue of hers. As the errant thought ran through his head so did the memory of what else that tongue could do, and Gideon had to force his mind out of the gutter lest the entire population of Halton see the effect she had on him.

"Am I truly not to be forgiven for a little subterfuge, Hope?" he asked quietly.

They separated before she could answer. And truth be told, she was so bloody stubborn that she probably wouldn't have answered at all. Gideon smiled politely at the young woman gazing up at him as they went through the motions of the dance, counting the seconds until he was with Hope again.

Finally, she was back in front of him, and he clasped her hand as they stepped toward each other, then back.

"You didn't answer my question," he said smoothly.

"Because I'm trying my best to ignore you," she sniped, her voice bitter. "Let go of my hand."

"No."

She narrowed her gaze.

"You're ruining the dance," she snapped.

"I don't care."

Her sigh sounded as though it came from the depths of her soul, and Gideon knew he was in very real danger of a black eye.

"You're making a scene," she tried again.

"I don't care."

Was that a growl?

He laughed softly at her obvious fury.

They were at the end of the line of dancers when he'd pulled them to a halt, so he knew they weren't interfering with the set. But he also knew they were drawing a lot of attention. Namely from Brentford, who was watching closely, and Francesca Templeworth, who again looked like she was about to go into battle.

"All I want is the chance to talk to you. To apologize."

"Why?"

Her question brought him up short. Not only because he was scared to examine his reasons but because she sounded genuinely curious. Not confrontational, not fed up. But genuinely baffled by why he was so insistent. And Gideon wasn't even sure he had an answer for her. All he knew for certain was that he hated that his past with Elaine had made him mistreat the beautiful woman standing before him now.

"What more is there to be said?"

And for some bizarre reason, her question immediately made Gideon defensive.

"I just, it was a simple misunderstanding. A bit of fun gone awry."

"Then why continue to speak of it? You are so determined to drag it on. Why?"

"Because I hurt you." His rigid self-control began to unravel. A mixture of guilt, desire, and contrition swirled in him. "And insane though it might be, nonsensical as it definitely is, it's killing me that I did so. And I want, no, I *need* to make amends."

"*Why?*" she demanded again, confusion filling the dark depths of her eyes. "Why does it matter so much?"

And Gideon couldn't only give her honesty.

"I don't know," he confessed quietly. "But it does."

HOPE CALLED HERSELF every type of fool for agreeing to come out here and be alone with Gideon. But he'd seemed so lost, she supposed, when he'd stopped their dance. The pain in his expression and his voice, well, perhaps she was more soft-hearted than she'd imagined because they'd been enough for her to agree to a walk.

The Assembly Rooms weren't equipped with verandas and gardens so their "walk" was actually limited to the courtyard and a small copse of trees to the left of it.

"That's where Elle and Christian first met, shall we say?" She smiled slightly at the memory.

She only brought it up because the silence was excruciating.

"Cheska had wandered out here with some gentleman or other, and Elodie, of course, came to the rescue. And Christian came to hers."

"And where were you when all of this happened?"

"I don't remember what I was doing, but I'm sure it was inappropriate."

He laughed, and Hope was surprised and a little concerned at the shiver of pleasure that skittered down her spine at the sound. This would not do. Not at all.

"I have no doubt. Though I cannot blame the viscount for wanting to rescue Lady Brentford. I was half tempted to fling that baron across the room when I saw him throw himself at you."

She didn't know what to say in response to such a thing, in response to the intimate tone of his voice. She, who never ran out of things to say, especially to a man, was rendered quite mute.

"Well, I didn't need rescuing," she rallied herself enough to quip. "In fact, I never *have* needed rescuing. Especially from a baron with an ego bigger than he is."

That laugh again. Oh heavens, she was in trouble. She needed to get out of here. Fast.

"I'm sure you haven't," he said quietly. "I couldn't help myself though. Besides, if it hadn't been me, I'm quite sure it would have been your sister."

"Cheska." She nodded. "Yes, quite. Though I'm confident that there would have been actual bloodshed if Cheska had gotten herself involved. She doesn't suffer gentlemen gladly."

"Nor should she."

"Indeed."

Silence descended again, though this time Hope couldn't think of a way to break it. She turned her back, gazing up at the cloudless sky and trying to convince her feet to turn around and leave.

"Kit and I, we went through a lot. Last year. Before my father died."

The gravity in his tone was so unexpected that it took Hope a moment to process the words. She turned back to see that he stalked closer to her. Now, only inches lay between them.

"There was a woman named Elaine. She was our stepmother."

Hope could only watch as he began to pace up and down for all the world like a panther in a cage.

"Though she didn't start out that way, and I didn't know about her and Kit before…"

Stopping abruptly, he turned and stared at her, gazing wordlessly into her eyes. She must have looked as confused as she felt, for he laughed softly, though there was no humor in the bleak sound, and ran a hand through his hair.

"I'm making a complete mess of this," he rasped. "I'm trying to apologize. And to explain. Because you're right, my behavior hurt you and that is the last thing I wanted to do. I have no excuses. I've allowed someone from my past to color my view so much that I didn't even realize it."

He drew to a stop again as though expecting her to answer, but Hope had no idea what to say.

"Gideon." She shrugged helplessly. "I don't know what to say. I don't understand what you're trying to tell me."

He merely gazed at her, and the longer they stood there, the more Hope's heart squeezed. And she knew without quite knowing *how* it had happened so quickly, that her heart was in very real danger of being lost to the earl who pretended not to be one. It was madness. But it was true.

When it didn't look as though he would speak again, Hope

stepped around him, meaning to go back inside and just wait for this interminable night to be over. But she'd hardly passed him when he reached out to stop her. She looked down at where he clasped her arm, watching the gooseflesh break out on her skin, then slowly back up to meet his eyes.

"I can accept your apology for whatever it's worth," she whispered. "But..."

"You didn't deserve my assumptions," he interrupted hoarsely. "And you were right. I did make them. About you. But not because of you. The truth is that my past experiences have made me a cynic. An utter bastard, to be blunt."

He paused as though she'd be shocked by his language. It was no different to her own. And Sophia had a mouth on her like a sailor.

"What happened, it's not something any of us speak of. But, well, I want you to know. For some reason, it's important to me that you know."

His words did nothing to ease her confusion, but they did pique her curiosity. And he looked so miserable, so desolate. She couldn't bear it. So, taking his large hand in her own, she led him to the back of the stables where she knew there was a quiet, secluded spot. The spot of her first kiss as a matter of fact. Not that he needed to know that particular tidbit.

They walked in silence, with Gideon seemingly happy to allow her to lead him. And when they sat, she reluctantly released his hand and turned to face him in the moonlight.

"Then tell me," she said softly.

So he did.

Chapter Fifteen

G IDEON'S HEAD THUMPED *as though someone had taken a damned anvil to it. Perhaps seeing his friends last night before heading straight to his father's far-more-respectable abode hadn't been the greatest idea.*

He turned to run his gaze along the silken skin of the woman whose bed he was currently in. Her raven hair was spilled across the snow-white pillows, the crips sheets doing little to hide her sensuous curves, and Gideon felt a stirring of desire.

Contemplating burying himself in her willing body once more before he took his leave, he sat up. But the pounding in his head only intensified and he decided to give it a miss. Besides, she didn't seem the type that would like him to outstay his welcome. Though she'd taken great pains to inform him that she was single and more than enthusiastic, she hadn't been in a place like that particular gaming hell because she was a virtuous miss.

And thank God for that. There were enough innocent misses filling the streets and houses of London every Season. Too many, in his opinion. Like Kit's paragon of virtue, Miss Samson, who had apparently become something of a nursemaid to their ailing father.

The woman beside him, whose name he was ashamed to say he couldn't remember, stirred and rolled to her side, pulling the counterpane over her and depriving him of the view. Just as well, he thought as he rolled the other way and began to dress in silence. He wasn't sure he'd be able to muster much enthusiasm with his head hurting.

The amount of brandy he'd drunk last night would have felled a lesser man. And truth be told, Gideon was rather impressed with himself that he'd managed anything in the lady's bedchamber given how foxed he'd felt.

He did wonder if he should wake her to at least say goodbye. Her home in Chelsea was modest but well-appointed, and though they hadn't exactly gotten to know each other, he could tell by her surroundings that she wasn't impoverished or of the serving classes.

Only a blackguard would sneak out without taking any sort of leave, he told himself fiercely. But perhaps that's exactly what he was. For within moments, he was out the door and hailing a hackney to Mayfair.

Well, what harm, he asked himself as he bounded up the stairs of the white stucco townhouse that had been in his family for decades. It wasn't as though he'd made the chit promises, and glancing at the longcase in the corner, he realized that it wouldn't be long until he'd be meeting his soon-to-be sister when Kit brought his Miss Samson home. So, putting the black-haired beauty from his mind, he called for a bath and one of his valet's magic concoctions to clear his head before putting on a show for the earl and Kit's fiancée. A couple of hours' worth of polite chit-chat and he'd be free to do whatever he wanted again.

G*IDEON WAS* F*LICKING* *through this morning's political news when he heard footsteps approaching.*

He hadn't seen Kit that morning, though he'd had a brief, strained meeting with the earl. His father's health wasn't remotely improved by the ministrations of Kit's Miss Samson, and Gideon had the vague, discomfiting thought that perhaps the old man wasn't long for this world. The earl had never exactly been the picture of doting fatherhood, but he was still Gideon's parent. The only one he had left, since his mother had succumbed to sickness when he'd been a mere child.

His somewhat maudlin thoughts were interrupted by the arrival of the butler to announce Kit's visitor. Gideon stood, feeling slightly annoyed that Kit was still holed up somewhere in the house and not here to greet his fiancée. But he knew that Jeffers would have already sent for

Kit.

So, pasting on as genuine a smile as he could muster through the remnants of a brandy-addled mind, he awaited the arrival of Kit's paragon.

The butler stepped back, and Gideon caught a glimpse of modest, violet skirts before looking up and straight into the face of the woman he'd tupped the night before.

Gideon felt his entire body go cold as he watched the woman curtsy, the picture of demure modesty. He knew she was anything but. The headache he'd been nursing all morning flared hot and painful and his stomach roiled sickeningly as he realized.

Surely it was some mistake. A vague memory from the night before floated through his racing mind.

"You know who I am?"

"I've only just learned…I admit, I was surprised to see just how handsome you are. I didn't think you would be."

She'd known. Last night she'd known that he was the Claremont heir. She'd known that he was Kit's damned brother. Gideon paid no attention as the butler bowed his way out of the room. His entire focus was on the woman standing before him, on the cold calculation in her blue eyes. On the asp-like smile on her lips. She'd known, and for whatever the hell reason, she'd not only kept it to herself, but she'd used him to cuckold his own brother.

"What the hell are you playing at?" he hissed when he could form a reasonably coherent sentence. "You knew last night who I was. That Kit was my brother?"

Her laugh was like claws on a chalkboard.

"Don't worry," she simpered. "Your brother will get over it soon enough."

Before Gideon could even guess what she was about, she threw herself into his arms.

"What…"

She pressed her lips against his in an open-mouthed kiss before he was able to push her away.

Gideon reached up and unwrapped her arms from his neck before pushing her firmly away.

"I don't know what you're about Miss Samson, but whatever it is, I *suggest you stop before Kit gets here."*

"Miss Samson?" Her laugh was as cold and cunning as the expression she wore. "I think we've become a little better acquainted than that, don't you?"

"Keep your hands to yourself," he snapped. "Whatever game this is to you, I can assure you, I won't be a part of it."

"You were a willing part of it last night, my lord," she purred, and damn it all to hell, but there was no denying she was the very embodiment of temptation. But Kit. Poor, foolish, trusting Kit.

Gideon gathered his anger, his guilt, and shame, and molded them into icy calm.

"Last night you were a willing light skirt, and I had time to kill," he said, his tone not betraying even a hint of the roiling anger beneath the surface. "This morning, you're no better than a Cyprian trying to betray a man who is far too good for you."

Her eyes narrowed as she took a slow, deliberate step back.

"I had thought to hang on for you, you know," she pouted. "Kit was a means to an end, of course. But once I saw you, well, it would be no hardship being your viscountess until it was time to be your countess. Far more palatable than the other option."

It took Gideon only seconds to realize what she meant. She'd throw over Kit for Gideon in the hopes that he'd marry her and be a means for her to claw her way to the top of the beau monde. And when that didn't work, she'd target their father. Gideon couldn't decide if she was insane or really just that greedy. Probably both. It shouldn't still surprise him what people were willing to do for money and a title. But this, this threw him, he'd admit. And now he had to figure out how to get her the hell away from his family, and how to tell his brother what he'd done.

"However, I can see that you're going to be difficult about this. What is it, some grand gesture of sibling loyalty? I thought you a tad more sophisticated than that, my lord," she laughed, and Gideon who'd never raised a hand in anger toward a woman, felt as though he could have happily wrung her neck. "But if you're going to be stubborn, then so be it. I'll revert to my original plan."

She was unhinged, Gideon thought. Utterly unhinged. And he was about to tell her so when the door to the drawing room banged open, heralding the arrival of another player in this farcical play. Not Kit, but the earl who, Gideon noticed with ever dawning horror, lit up the second he spied the woman standing in the middle of the room.

"My dear Elaine," his father rasped. "I thought that might be you."

Gideon watched, horrified, as she turned a sweet, demure smile on his father.

"How are you this morning, my lord? I was just getting acquainted with your son. Shall we take our walk?"

Gideon could only watch, struck dumb by the little harlot's audacity as she hurried over and draped her arm through his father's.

"They've been taking daily walks," Jeffers suddenly whispered to Gideon, who turned to frown down at the older man. There was a world of warning in the butler's usually stoic face. "They are quite the highlight of his lordship's day, my lord."

The implication in the words were horrifying.

"Does Kit know?"

"He knows that Miss Samson is attentive to your father," Jeffers hedged. "But then your brother has always seen the best in people. Even if they don't deserve it."

It was the most forward Gideon could ever remember the old servant being. And it was a testament to the stranglehold Miss Samson had on the members of his family that the butler would speak out so frankly now.

Whatever the hell she was up to, Gideon knew he had to stop it. But first, he'd have to confess to Kit what he'd done.

"As it turned out, I was too late."

He felt raw, emotionally drained. He hadn't spoken about this since their father had passed away last year, and he'd had to deal with his widow.

"Kit, being the person he is, didn't blame me. Not that he had to, for I blamed myself enough for the both of us. I felt disgusted. Ashamed. So *angry* with Elaine, yes, but with myself, too. But though Kit cried off immediately, she'd already sunk her claws into my elder, ailing father. They were married within weeks of the end of her engagement to Kit. Despite our protestations, despite what people would think. The old fool just didn't care. Didn't care about what she'd done to Kit, how she'd used me, how he would hurt his own son. They married, and she got what she wanted, to become a countess and be a very wealthy woman."

Hope hadn't spoken throughout his humiliating tale. Hadn't breathed even from what he heard, save for her gasp of shock at this last, embarrassing piece of the awful jigsaw.

"I couldn't stand it. Stand to be around my father or Elaine. Not even Kit. Not after what I'd done. So, I left. Traveled the Continent for a while, stayed with friends. Six months later, my father was dead. Even better for Elaine, really. Title, wealth, and no old husband to pretend to give a damn about. She took off before his funeral. We haven't seen or heard from her since. Her solicitor dealt with mine. My father had changed his will the day after they were wed. She received property in Evesham, some of the Claremont jewels, and a monthly stipend."

"Where is she now?" Hope asked, her voice flat.

Gideon's gut twisted. Was she so disgusted then? He'd never heard her sound so icy. He risked a look at her and saw that while her voice might be frigid, the fire in her eyes was anything but. And, he realized with a start, something warm expanding in his chest, it didn't seem to be aimed at him.

"I don't know." He shrugged. Suddenly, the weight of Elaine's actions didn't seem all that heavy anymore. "The last we heard she had sold the property and moved on. Her stipend is paid to solicitors in Ireland. We have no contact with her."

"I've never heard of her," Hope said now. "Even in London, she's never been seen, has she?"

"No, not that I know of. She didn't keep very high company before she became entangled with my brother and then married my father. And of course, when the scandal broke, she must have known she wouldn't be accepted anywhere. Wherever she is, I'm sure she's relishing playing lady of the manor. But it would have to be somewhere far enough away that the scandal wouldn't chase her."

He drew to a halt, not quite sure what to say now. Not even sure why it had been so important to him that she know it all. He expected that she'd get up and leave now. Why would she want to entangle herself in such madness? And did he even want her to?

His thoughts stopped dead along with his heart as she reached out a hand and clasped his own.

"She's a vile old trout," Hope said stoutly, and he couldn't help but laugh. Nobody could ever accuse her of being afraid to speak her mind. And her honesty was something that he realized was a precious commodity. Something that made him feel even guiltier for his own subterfuge.

"My stepmother almost tore my family apart, Hope," he said, the words feeling as though they were dredged from a long-forgotten part of himself. "And she made it almost impossible for me to trust. To care."

He swallowed, and his heart sped alarmingly, though he couldn't have said why.

"Until now," he finally grated. "Until you."

Chapter Sixteen

HOPE HAD HAD her first kiss right here when she'd been thirteen years old. Not much of a kiss mind. Just enough for her to know that perhaps boys weren't *quite* as disgusting as she'd assumed.

It had been the only kiss she'd ever initiated. The only one she'd ever taken. Cheska had dared her that she wouldn't be brave enough to do it and so what choice had she had but to grab hold of the poor, unsuspecting stable boy and squash his lips with her own. In hindsight, it had probably been her own fault that it hadn't been very good.

Perhaps it was Providence that brought her back here now. Because for the second time in her life, she was going to kiss someone instead of waiting to be kissed.

Gideon's awful story, that terrible guilt that she didn't feel he deserved to carry, it broke her heart. And while she still wasn't exactly thrilled that he'd thought her as awful as his stepmother, she had to repress a shudder at even the thought of the distasteful situation. She could understand how something like that could change a person. Color his perception of things. Distrust women, even.

But beyond all that, there was simply no denying the attraction she still felt toward him. Moreso now that she knew his tragic tale. She'd already known how fond he was of his brother. Just as she knew how genuinely kind-hearted Kit Bell was. So, to hear that he'd been used and treated so abominably, that they both had, well, truth be told, if Elaine Samson, or Bell she supposed, had been standing in front of her right now, Hope would have happily scratched the other woman's eyes out! Not only for her actions then but for the embarrassment Gideon still clearly felt. She vaguely remembered Christian mentioning some sort of scandal. But her brother-in-law hadn't seemed to remember or care what it had been. But then, Christian had caused his own share of scandal in the past, so perhaps he just didn't think it noteworthy.

A gentle summer breeze swept around them, and she watched in a sort of rapt fascination as a lock of sable hair fell across Gideon's brow.

Until now. Until you.

Such simple words, yet Hope couldn't help but feel that they shifted something between them.

She should leave, of course. Get up and go back inside. Forgive him for his harsh, misguided opinions, thank him for his honesty, and then return to the ball. Dance with the gentlemen with whom she always danced. Talk with the ladies with whom she had little to nothing in common.

Suddenly, the very idea was abhorrent. And Hope knew that she wasn't going to go anywhere because she couldn't think of a single place she would want to be rather than right here. With Gideon.

Without quite knowing what she was about, she lifted a hand and brushed the lock of hair back from his brow. When she made to take her hand back, he reached up and grasped hold of it, pressing it against his face before turning and placing a single, tender kiss in the center of her palm.

And that one, simple action was all the encouragement Hope needed. A voice that sounded suspiciously like Elodie's told her that she was on precarious ground for a whole host of reasons. But when had Hope ever listened to Elodie? When had she ever cared a jot for sense or propriety?

And why on earth would she start now?

Moving on pure instinct, she slid her hand down to wrap around the nape of his neck. She caught one, fleeting look at the blaze of desire that suddenly lit the dark depths of his eyes before her lips made contact with his own. And any chance of coherent thought was lost as she was flung into a maelstrom of pure feeling.

IT TOOK ONLY seconds, perhaps even less, for the ever-present desire that Gideon constantly fought to repress to flare to life as Hope leaned forward and pressed that torturous, smart mouth against his own.

And even less time for him to take control of the kiss with a growl of pure, masculine need. She would ruin him, Gideon knew. If she let him, he would take and take and take what he wanted and destroy anyone who got in the way of it.

His desire was a live thing coursing through his veins which only burned hotter at her soft, maddening moans. Plunging his tongue inside her mouth to dance with her own, he reached out and lifted her bodily from the seat beside him, draping her across his lap instead.

The feel of her soft, pliant body against his rigid cock had them both groaning simultaneously, and Gideon thought he might burst right there on the spot. She writhed against him, the pleasure of her actions bordering on pain, and Gideon ripped his mouth from hers to hiss against her throat.

"Christ, Hope. You'll be the death of me," he rasped, pressing a trail of hot kisses along her neck to her ear.

"Likewise," she whispered, dragging a breathless laugh from him.

He pressed his forehead against her own, willing himself to calm down, willing his blood to cool. But Hope, it seemed, had different ideas, for she grasped his face between her delicate hands and dragged it up toward her own again.

"Don't stop," she said.

But he needed to. God, he'd never heard anything so sweet as her request for him to continue. But he needed to stop. Because he wasn't sure he'd have the strength to in a moment.

"Hope, sweetheart, I…"

She didn't give him a chance to continue. Choosing instead to boldly press her lips to his once more. And the last, shredded vestige of his control burned away in the flame of desire.

Digging his hands into her carefully coiffed hair, Gideon couldn't contain his growl of satisfaction as the caramel locks came undone and tumbled through his fingers in a waterfall of floral-scented silk.

He knew that if he lived to be a hundred, he would never smell anything as tempting as the scent of Hope Templeworth. She wiggled against him, and it took Herculean strength—a strength he'd never known he possessed—not to lift her skirts and bury himself inside her there and then.

But she deserved more, so much more than that. And for all her natural seductiveness, he knew she was an innocent and needed to be treated as such. Still, she'd bloody test the patience of a saint.

Once again, Gideon pulled his mouth from her to catch an earlobe between his teeth. Damn, but was there any part of her that didn't taste as good as she looked? He'd never get enough. She would become an obsession, more addictive than any substance, more necessary than even the air he breathed. And some small part of him was terrified of the thought and all it entailed. But the rest of him was too busy being ravenous for her to care.

She arched against him, straining her long, elegant neck to give him better access, and he took full advantage, driving them both crazy by pulling her even closer to the rigid pulse of his desire.

"Gideon." His name on her lips was a plea and a prayer. "Please," she gasped, her pulse fluttering frantically at the base of her throat. "Please."

"You'll be the death of me," he snarled against that maddening pulse. "But I can't think of a better way to go."

Her laugh, breathless as it was, sent a jolt of pleasure through not just his enflamed body but his heart, too. And he realized that he liked making her laugh. Wanted to make her smile.

What the hell is this? he asked himself. He was drawn to her fire, her sass. Her beauty, yes, but also that feistiness that drove him half-mad with exasperation and longing all at the same time.

She'd bewitched him. It was as simple and as terrifying as that.

A whimper escaped her throat as though she was burning with the same need as he. And smug bastard that he was, he couldn't help but rejoice in the sound even as it sent his own yearning up a notch.

He felt like he was about to combust just from touching her. And he hadn't even begun to explore the curves and slopes of the body that had filled his dreams and fueled his fantasies from that first meeting at the lake.

The memory sent his hands moving almost of their own accord, and Gideon reveled in every gasp, every moan he wrenched from her lips. The first swipe of a hand from her throat to her waist set her arching even more, and he took full advantage, reaching up to cup one full, heavy breast in his palm.

His guttural sound of satisfaction melded with her own as he ran a thumb slowly over the nipple that peaked even under the silk of her gown. It wasn't enough, he decided as he moved to capture her lips once again in a bruising kiss. It was nowhere near enough.

Without thought to the fact that they were on a damned bench out in the open, that anyone could walk by and see them, Gideon reached inside the neckline of the gown, further still until he'd wrenched aside the chemise, his hand on her flesh.

Somewhere in the background of his frantic thoughts, he heard the distinctive sound of ripping material. But he didn't give a damn. He'd buy every chemise from here to India if it meant he could touch her like this.

He wanted to plunge beneath her skirts and claw at her like a wild animal, but he paced himself, drawing out the pleasure and the pain for them both. Running his hand up the muscled smoothness of her calves, he kept going until…

His black oath was muffled against her breast as he touched the impossibly soft skin of her bare thigh. She was moving her hips now in shameless abandon. It was the most exquisite torture he'd ever endured. He could take her right here, right now. And she would not object.

He could give them both what they wanted, marry her afterward, and make her his forever.

The thought came thundering through his head and for a split second, Gideon felt nothing but panic. What the hell was he thinking? He'd known her a couple of weeks at most. Kissed her twice. What sort of lunatic did it make him to be thinking that way?

He was about ready to put an end to this madness. To put some much-needed distance between himself and the temptation Hope presented and just *think*. But the feel of her, the sound of her, the *taste* of her.

Gideon knew he could no more stop this now than he could steal the stars from the heavens.

The thigh still in his grip began to tremble as he edged ever closer to the core of her. He'd be walking around in discomfort for days after this, he thought wryly. Because as much as he knew he was in the throes of madness, he would never actually take her on a bloody bench.

But they didn't both need to suffer. And he knew he would get untold pleasure from feeling her come completely undone in his arms. From knowing that *he* was the one bringing her pleasure. *His* were the arms that held her.

And as that possessive arrogance took root, he finally reached her center and relished in her gasp.

"Gideon!"

He looked up, and the look of heated wonder in those eyes took his breath away.

"I want to feel…"

He brushed a kiss against her mouth. "I know, sweetheart," he whispered against her lips. Deepening the kiss, he pressed his thumb against her center, and almost exploded at the sound of sheer longing that poured into his mouth. He swallowed the sound, knowing it would wreak havoc on his senses later when he was alone and remembering every exquisite second of this.

He couldn't help the curse that spilled from his own lips as he slowly dipped a finger inside of her, feeling her clench around him as he drove them both mad with his mouth and his hands.

She moved against his hand with ever-growing abandon, and he knew she was close to the edge. He bent his head to her breast once more and bit gently as he pressed his thumb harder against her flesh.

And there it was.

She cried his name, and he coaxed her through every stunning second of her release, watching in rapt fascination the changing expressions on her face. Wonder, awe, and unadulterated ecstasy.

He'd never seen anything so beautiful. He never would again.

The silence that descended on them when her body stilled was filled with everything he knew he wouldn't say to her. Not yet. Not until he could figure out his jumbled thoughts, his mangled heart.

He wondered if she knew. As he gazed at her in the moonlight, her hair unbound and surrounding her face like a halo, he wondered if she knew that she was very close to being the center of his world.

He wondered if he could handle such a thing, let alone her.

The silence stretched on, and damned if he knew how to

break it. Perhaps she would regret what they'd done. Perhaps she would decide that she was too angry, still, to forgive him, or that his behavior in the past, his entanglement with Elaine, and the mess it had made of him would be something that she couldn't forgive and couldn't get past.

But as he watched, struck dumb by her beauty, she smiled. Softly and a little shellshocked still. But it was a definite smile. And it was the most wonderful thing he'd ever seen.

Happiness and something delicate and impossibly tender rushed through him at that smile, and he could only return it with one of his own.

"I..."

"Hope?"

A female voice suddenly rent the air, and Hope froze in his arms, her eyes widening in alarm.

"Hope! I have absolutely no doubt that you're out here, and you have five seconds to get in front of me."

"Love, why don't we..."

"Hush, Christian."

"Right you are."

Hope scrambled off Gideon's lap and shoved to her feet, shaking out her skirts, then patting frantically at her hair, her gaze darting around them, no doubt looking for the pins that he'd knocked from her curls.

"Hope Mariah Templeworth. If you do not come out *right now* I shall..."

"Elodie, look. There's that copse of trees. That very spot is where I fell in love with you."

"Hope! You are, wait, what?"

Gideon listened in some amusement as the viscountess went from scolding governess to simpering miss in an instant.

The viscount was good, he'd give him that, Gideon thought as he calmly bent and gathered up the missing hairpins.

"You did not," Lady Brentford scoffed, and Gideon wanted to kiss Brentford's feet for doing an excellent job of distracting his wife. "It took you an age to fall in love with me."

"No, love. It took me an age to *admit* that I'd fallen in love with you. But show me the man who wouldn't lose his heart to you after you'd tackled him to the ground and flung herself on top of him."

The viscountess's laugh rang through the courtyard.

"I didn't tackle you, you cad! And I certainly didn't…"

Her words were cut off in an instant, and Gideon could only guess the reason. Guess at it and be fiercely jealous of it.

He looked back at Hope. She'd hurriedly pinned her hair, though the style was a lot less intricate than the one she'd arrived with. And though, she still looked every inch the lady, she also looked slightly disheveled and thoroughly kissed. That masculine smugness reared its head again, as did the aching desire for her.

"I should probably sneak back in," she whispered. "Before Christian's obvious distraction tactics stop working."

They shared a conspiratorial grin.

"It might be prudent for you to wait awhile. Before returning, too," she said hesitantly as though she was unsure of what she should do or say. Well, that made two of them.

"I'll wait and slip in the back," he said, and he might have imagined it, but he thought he caught a fleeting hint of disappointment in her eyes. Could it be that she wanted to return with him? That she wanted people to know they'd been together?

He couldn't even begin to think his way around that possibility. Not when his mind and body were already in turmoil. But nor could he have her thinking that he was in any way ashamed of what had just happened here.

Before she could run off, he reached out and clasped her hands.

"Am I forgiven enough now for you to actually speak to me if I call? Or will you hide away for another three days?"

She narrowed her eyes at him, but there was that mischief that he loved lurking in the deep brown depths.

"I might deign to see you," she sniffed. "Unless I get a better offer."

She was a little tearaway. And she'd drive him mad, he knew, before he left this insane town.

But for the first time in two years, he felt real, genuine happiness.

"What if I up my offer to a picnic? Do you think something better than that will come along before tomorrow?"

She kept him waiting while she pretended to consider it. At least, he hoped she was pretending!

Finally, he was rewarded with that dimpled smile.

"Fine. A picnic. And I happen to know a great spot, right by the lake."

Just like that, Gideon's blood heated to a boiling point, but before he could do anything about it, the viscountess's voice sounded once more.

"Hope! That's it."

The distinct sound of feet stomping on gravel signaled the end of the viscount's distraction efforts, and before Gideon could blink, Hope was gone in a flurry of skirts. Gideon stood there trying to catch his breath and put the earth back on its axis. There was a moment or two of silence before…

"There she is! Hope, what on earth have you been up to?"

"Nothing you want to know about," Hope called airily, and Gideon laughed, rubbing at the peculiar but not unpleasant ache in his chest.

Chapter Seventeen

"WELL, YOU DEFINITELY got up to *something* last night. There's an air about you."

Hope rolled her eyes at Francesca's suspicious statement. She was exhausted enough as it was without the interrogation. Sleep had, unsurprisingly, eluded her last night, and she'd spent the night tossing and turning before drifting off as the birds began to chirp. Even then, her dreams had been filled with memories of Gideon and that mouth and those hands…

They'd spent most of the morning having the same conversation over and over again. And now, they had apparently decided to start up again, even though she was trying her best to ignore them all by pretending to read her novel.

"See? She's gone all funny again."

Hope scowled at Sophia, who was now watching her suspiciously, too.

"I just didn't sleep very well last night," Hope said as calmly as she could, though her heart was racing. In truth, her entire world had shifted last night. She'd allowed Gideon to take liberties that Elodie and Christian would probably lock her up for. Yet, she could not bring herself to regret it.

The problem, she'd decided at some point in the never-ending night, was that she suspected she'd gone and fallen in love with the man, which was, of course, a disaster. For a whole host of reasons. Namely that he had given no indication that he felt the same way, he had expressed no wish to marry and made her no promises, and given his past and what that odious woman had done to his entire family, he wasn't likely to ever trust someone enough to open his heart to her.

She heaved a sigh that felt as though it came from the depths of her soul before noticing that everyone's focus was still on her. Cheska's in particular.

Francesca had always had an odd ability to tell when any of them was lying, and Sophia would just stir up trouble whenever and however she could. Hope looked to Elodie and Christian, for once wanting one of her older sister's lectures about proper conversation. But to her horror, Elle was gazing avidly at her, with Christian looking almost as suspicious as Cheska.

"You were out there with *someone* Hope. And I have a fairly good guess as to who that might have been."

Hope shrugged her shoulders, feigning a nonchalance she didn't quite feel.

"You do? For the life of me, I can't remember which of my admirers it was. Perhaps you can give me a clue?"

Christian's growl indicated that her brother-in-law might not be all that entertained by her quip, and she smiled sweetly, batting her lashes.

"Funny, Hope," he drawled. But then his eyes hardened slightly as he sat back, draping an arm over the back of Elle's chair. "You know, I couldn't help but notice that Claremont seemed to go missing around the same time as you did. Right after your dance, as a matter of fact."

"Is that so?" she asked. "How curious."

"Hope…"

A knock sounded from the front door, and they all froze.

Hope darted her eyes to the longcase clock. It was early for afternoon callers but only just. Mama was paying her own calls today, and Papa was touring the estate with his steward. Not that their father received callers, of course.

Her heart began pounding, her stomach a riot of butterflies.

She tried to school her features into a look of casual disinterest but wasn't sure that anyone was fooled by it.

There was the sound of a quick, muffled conversation before the distinctive noise of a servant heading her way. Hope didn't know quite what to do with herself as she watched the door, all pretense of innocence beyond her now. She wasn't even sure that she was blinking, truth be told.

A quick rap, a push of the oak door, and there was Stevens with his silver tray, a rectangle calling card set perfectly in the middle of it. Hope stared at the card, noticing in her periphery that everyone else did so, too.

"Lord Claremont, my lord, my lady, Miss Hope."

Hope's heart stopped dead in her chest before restarting at a gallop that she was fairly sure could kill her. She'd known he was coming, of course. Had agreed to picnic with him today. But, unbidden the image of their embrace last night, the things he'd done to her, the evidence of his own desire that she'd felt. It all came clamoring back whilst she stood there. With almost her entire family. All of whom were already suspicious. And to her horror, she felt her cheeks heat dramatically and knew that they must be scarlet.

They all stood staring at each other, then at the card, then at each other again, then at the confused servant. None of them moved. None of them spoke.

"Ah, sh-should I tell the gentleman you are not at home?" Stevens asked, his tone vaguely baffled.

"No!"

Well, that did it. Hope cringed slightly as all faces turned to her, following her little outburst with varying, not particularly pleasant to look at expressions. Cheska looked more suspicious than ever; Sophia was smirking. Elle looked perhaps a little misty-eyed, and Christian looked ready to rip someone's head off. All in all, she would have preferred to have been alone.

"Send him in, Stevens," Elodie said calmly, her tone dulcet and ladylike.

Hope stood on shaking legs, placing her book on the chaise behind her. Her yellow skirts swirled around her feet, and she wondered for perhaps the fiftieth time that morning if she should have picked something else to wear.

But she thought she looked well enough. The gown was simple in its design, its only adornment white piping along the bodice and capped sleeves. She'd matched it with a plain, white ribbon in her hair and would wear a simple white redingote for their picnic.

That was, of course, if they made it out of here alive.

The butler bowed before stepping aside, and then, there he was. Hope felt her breath catch as Gideon strode confidently into the room. He looked as handsome today as he had last night in more formal wear. His green superfine was perfectly fitted, and she knew that his large, muscled frame needed no padding in the material. She couldn't help but run her eyes over him, the fawn breeches snug against his legs, the shiny black Hessians, the snow-white lawn shirt and cravat. Everything fit him so well. *Beautiful* didn't seem the correct word to use for someone so masculine. But handsome simply didn't do him justice.

She raised her eyes back to his face and saw with a start that he'd been watching her watching him. And her cheeks grew hotter still at the knowing, vaguely smug look in his eyes. But along with that smugness there was desire. Perhaps even tenderness.

"Claremont, what brings you here this afternoon?"

Christian's question seemed to break the spell between Hope and Gideon, and she found herself having to blink rapidly a few times to focus on her surroundings. She caught Elodie's expression and remembered herself in time to roll her eyes at her sister's knowing smile.

"Brentford." Gideon took the viscount's extended hand in a firm grip, and the ladies could only watch as the handshake went on...and on...neither gentleman letting go, each seeming to size the other up.

Hope had no idea what was going on, and from the looks of things, neither did her sisters. It was starting to get uncomfortable when Cheska suddenly snorted.

"Wouldn't it be quicker to just measure your…"

"Lord Claremont," Elodie interrupted whatever scandalous thing Cheska was going to say.

Hope couldn't stifle her laughter. Elodie looked most disapproving. Sophia, thankfully, still looked confused. Hope didn't miss the twitch of amusement on Gideon's face or the blatant grin on Christian's.

"How kind of you to call. Will you take tea with us?" Elodie asked.

Gideon had no choice but to end the odd stand-off with Christian to answer Elle's question. He released Christian's hand and bowed politely to Elodie, the portrait of a sophisticated gentleman.

"You are very kind, my lady, but I'm afraid I cannot stay long. I was hoping that Miss Hope was free this afternoon and would consent to take a ride in my gig."

His words were perfectly innocent, but when his eyes alighted on hers, the look in them was anything but. Lord, if her cheeks kept heating like this, she'd likely catch fire! Hope did her best to school her features into a mask of blasé politeness.

"Thank you, my lord," Hope said.

"I'm not sure that's such a good idea," Christian spoke up, eyeing Hope and Gideon carefully.

Hope raised a brow in the viscount's direction.

"Thankfully, your opinion on the matter isn't required," she said, her voice deceptively soft. She had no idea why Christian had chosen now to play the overprotective man of the house, but it wouldn't be to Hope's detriment, that was for sure.

He opened his mouth, probably to argue, and she decided that she simply wouldn't give him the chance.

"Let's go," she said to Gideon, reaching out to grab his hand and pull him bodily from the room.

"Hope!" Elodie sounded exasperated but resigned behind her. "When will you be back?"

"I have no idea," she called gaily as she took her redingote and straw bonnet from her grinning abigail on the way out the door. And she didn't stop until they were standing in front of a lacquered gig and two gorgeous grays.

"Oh, Sophia would simply die for your horses," Hope said as she plonked her bonnet on her head. "In fact, I suggest we get out of here right now before she gets wind of them, otherwise we'll never get away."

"Your family are…"

"I know," she interrupted before he could finish. She could quite easily guess at what he would say. She'd heard any number of less than complimentary descriptions over the years. Though Gideon, to his credit, seemed more amused than put off by them. "And you caught them on a good day," she continued, trying to ignore her sudden nervousness at his close proximity.

This close to him, she could see the flecks of gold in his impossibly dark eyes. She could smell the sandalwood and soap coming from his skin. She could practically feel the heat of his body. And it all reminded her of last night. What he'd done. What she'd done. How much she wanted more. How he had shattered her, filled her with ecstasy while still leaving her somehow aching and craving more.

Perhaps that made her the hussy that the town biddies had oft accused her of being. Perhaps she should be ashamed of such wanton thoughts and desires. But standing here in the sunlight with him, she couldn't bring herself to care.

And yet, there was an awkwardness that she couldn't quite rid herself of. She didn't know if she should bring up what happened last night, didn't even know *could* bring it up without expiring from embarrassment. And so, all she managed to do was stand there mutely like a dolt staring up at him.

She didn't know if Gideon suffered the same affliction, but he did stand there and stare right back, so it was possible. He gazed at her for what felt like forever before his lips quirked into a hint of a smile.

"You look ravishing," he said softly.

And even though Hope had heard variations of such things hundreds of times from countless men in her life, she felt herself blush with pleasure. Perhaps it was because he seemed so sincere. But, she suspected, it was because he was the only man she'd ever met whose opinions were important to her. She *wanted* him to mean it. She wanted to be attractive to him. And because of that, she couldn't seem to muster any of her usual flippancy or even faux conceit. All she could do was answer his smile with a beaming one of her own.

He shook his head slightly as though clearing it before his expression turned wry.

"I don't think I've ever been struck dumb by a lady before, Hope Templeworth. You hold a concerning amount of power in that smile of yours," he quipped.

"Me?" she trilled innocently, though secretly she was warmed by his words.

"Yes, you," he grumbled good-naturedly as he reached out to wrap his hands around her waist. "It should be weaponized."

His hands were warm and almost spanned her waist with their size, and Hope couldn't stop the hitch in her breathing at the contact. His gaze flew to hers at the sound, and where once amusement had danced in their depths, now there was only fire. And Hope's blood immediately heated in response.

"Hope."

"Oh, look at his horses! I knew they'd be beautiful. Lord Claremont, can I see them?"

"Damn it."

Gideon, instead of being horrified for even surprised, merely laughed at Hope's language as they both turned to see Sophia bounding down the steps of the manor house toward them, legs clad, unsurprisingly, in breeches, hair flying out behind her.

"Later, Sophia," Hope said as she stepped subtly out of Gideon's grip, telling herself it was idiotic to miss the feel of his hands around her. "We're leaving now."

"Are you?" Sophia drawled. "Because it looked like you were standing there making moon eyes at each other. I could have taken care of the horses until you were done."

Hope could happily wring her little sister's neck at least once a day. Apparently, this was today's event.

"Go away," she sniped embarrassment, sharpening her tone. She didn't want her sisters thinking she was out here making *moon eyes* at a man. She had something of a reputation to maintain, after all. Hope was the one about whom men simpered. It was very much *not* supposed to be the other way around.

"Well, is he coming back?" Sophia crossed her arms, refusing to move. "Because you said I could examine them later. So, is he coming back here after your ride?"

Lord, but Hope could murder her. She turned to glance apologetically at Gideon who must think they were all raving lunatics. But he was all easy smiles as he turned to Sophia.

"Why Miss Templeworth, that sounded very much like an invitation to dine. And I shall be delighted to accept, thank you."

Sophia narrowed her eyes at him as though working out whether she'd been tricked or not. But after a moment, she shrugged.

"I don't particularly care what you eat, as long as you let me at your horses." She grinned, then without a word of farewell, marched toward the stables.

Gideon laughed as he turned back to Hope and lifted her easily into his gig.

"Should I be concerned that of almost all my interactions with you and your sisters, that conversation was amongst the politest?"

Hope laughed, her heart fit to burst.

"Consider yourself lucky then," she said as he climbed in beside her and took up the reins. "You're obviously growing on us."

Chapter Eighteen

GIDEON FELT A little shellshocked from his brief visit with the Templeworth clan. Of course, he'd met them all before but not after he'd seduced one of them in a public courtyard.

He'd spent most of last night torn between desperation for the woman beside him and confusion as to whether or not he should feel guilty. Then of course he'd taken one look at her this morning and guilt was the furthest thing from his mind.

He'd meant what he'd said, too, about that smile. It was dangerous. Everything about her was dangerous. And he didn't give a damn. It didn't stop him from wanting to be with her every second of every day. He was fast on the way to being utterly infatuated with the lady. And he was only partially terrified by the idea.

She'd said he was growing on them. And Gideon had been surprised by how happy such an innocuous comment had made him. He could only hope that she included herself in that group. Manipulating his way into a dinner invitation probably wasn't the best way to conduct himself but, in his defense, not a lot of rules seemed to apply to the Templeworth women. At least, not any that they cared about.

Even Brentford was a decent sort. Gideon hadn't spent a lot of time in Town after the disaster that was Elaine Samson's presence in their lives, and the fallout from her marriage to the late earl. But he did know that Brentford hadn't been one of the gossipers around the debacle. Hadn't shunned any of them when others did. Though, now that he'd gotten to know the man's family, he could only guess that the viscount had had his hands full with the little hoydens and probably didn't have the time to even know about anyone else's drama, let alone gossip about it.

But he *liked* them, Gideon realized. He liked their blatant disregard for propriety. He liked their banter, their wicked sense of humor, and their irreverence for the stuffy world they lived in. And he liked that underneath the bickering and madness, they loved each other fiercely and took care of each other. That's how things should be. That's how things should have been with him and Kit.

Yes, he'd always looked out for his little brother. But if they'd been closer, if Gideon hadn't kept his life as separate to Kit's and his father's as possible, Elaine never would have been able to do what she did.

"You don't have to, you know."

Hope's gentle voice mercifully interrupted his thoughts before they could grow too maudlin. He didn't want his mistakes, his complicated past, casting a shadow over this day.

"I don't have to what?" he asked as he steered his grays toward the road that would lead them past her father's formal gardens and toward the meadows beyond.

"Stay to dinner," she responded. "You can't let Sophia bully you. Once you give in, well, just ask Christian."

Gideon laughed softly.

"It would take a braver man than I not to bring these horses back to her, I'm afraid." He shuddered, only half feigning the terror. "But if it would displease or inconvenience you..."

"It won't" she answered quickly before smiling gently. "It won't displease me."

He couldn't tear his eyes away from her, and the silence between them began to fill with that magic that always seemed to surround them.

Hope heaved a sigh before dragging her gaze away. And he

missed them on her, like some sort of love-addled sop.

"Besides, there's no getting out of it now. Not just because of Sophia. But when Mama finds out an *earl* is coming to dinner!" She paused and rolled her eyes, and Gideon was left to wonder how he could ever have thought she'd care about his title when she seemed so singularly unimpressed with it. "I just hope she restocked her smelling salts. She went through tons of the stuff when she found out Christian was going to be her son-in-law."

Gideon barked a laugh, the sound foreign to his own ears. It had been so long, too long, since he'd laughed like this.

"Well at least one of the Templeworth ladies is duly impressed with me," he drawled. "The rest of you could turn impudence into a sport."

She shrugged, marvelously unperturbed by his observation.

"I've yet to meet the gentleman who couldn't benefit from being taken down to size every now and again," she purred innocently. "My sisters and I consider it something of a civic duty."

Gideon could only laugh again. She was incorrigible. Trouble down to her very core. Irascible, irreverent, a proud rule-breaker.

And she was fast becoming someone he was afraid he wouldn't want to live without. The thought sent something akin to panic scurrying along his veins. In two weeks, maybe three if he pushed it, he would be returning to his main seat to oversee the harvest and preparations for winter and next spring.

He'd planned to leave Halton and not come back. Perhaps every year or so to check in with Kit considering a vicar couldn't exactly head home over Christmastide. A busy time for a vicar, after all.

So, would that be it then? Would he pack up his meager belongings and leave Halton, leave Hope behind?

"Here we are."

Once again, her chipper voice interrupted his musings, and he realized that he had in fact driven them to the lake.

And just like that, the memory of that day, of her wet, near-naked body, slammed into him, and he had to hurry to stop the horses lest he drive them straight into the bloody water. The air seemed to crackle between them once more as every worry, every panicked thought, every *coherent* thought emptied from his head.

"Gideon."

That was it. That one, breathless sound of his name on her lips was all it took for his tenuous control to snap. Gideon reached out, pulled her bonnet from her head, and clasped her face between his hands. He gave her a second to stop him, praying that she wouldn't. Then those incredible eyes, eyes that had haunted him from the first moment he'd looked into them, closed, and it was all the permission he needed.

The kiss was no bruising clash of passions. No explosion of desire. But no less earth-shattering for it. He poured every confusing thought, every unnamed emotion into it, coaxing her lips open with a brush of his tongue, exploring her mouth, and reveling in every sigh, every tiny moan that drove him wild.

He felt her reach out and grasp the lapels of his jacket as he angled her head to deepen the embrace. Felt her capitulation to the very depths of his soul. He could do this forever, he realized. Just hold her and kiss her and be alone with her.

A sudden, an obnoxious squawk interrupted them, and they broke apart as though a firework exploded between them. Her giggle was quite possibly the most beautiful sound Gideon had ever heard.

Christ, if his friends from the gaming hells could hear this romantic tosh, they wouldn't believe it. He wouldn't have believed himself even capable of feeling such romantic tosh, truth be told. But like so much of his life, Hope had changed that.

Throwing her a rueful grin, he quickly jumped from the gig and then threw the reins over the branch of a tree hanging over the water before turning back to lift her from the conveyance. But she was way ahead of him. He could only watch as she hitched up her skirts, giving him the most tantalizing view of stocking-clad legs before she jumped, agile as a cat, and landed on her feet.

Shaking out her skirts, she turned and dragged the picnic basket he'd had Cook prepare that morning, and the blanket he'd packed himself from the bag of the gig. Then, turning back to face him, she held them both out. His hands moved automatically to take them from his grasp.

"Come along then," she said, the slightly husky tone in her voice addling his brain further. "I know the perfect spot for a picnic."

She spun around and stalked off toward the edge of the lake, clearly expecting him to follow her. And of course, he did.

HOPE HURRIED AHEAD of Gideon, praying that her racing heart would calm by the time they reached the secluded spot she'd decided on for their picnic.

That kiss, the way he'd made her feel the second his hands had touched her face, if nothing else, proved that the feelings he'd awakened in her last night hadn't been a fluke. She hadn't been carried away by the daringness of it, or the two glasses of champagne she'd consumed. It had been him. Just him.

She could hear twigs snapping beneath his feet behind her, so she knew he was following. Not that she'd given him much of a choice, of course. But she knew the area like the back of her hand, and the spot she had in mind was perfect for a picnic. And for some privacy. Privacy that she suspected would be very much needed since he couldn't seem to keep his hands off her, and she couldn't seem to want him to.

Spotting the willow that she was aiming for ahead of her, Hope turned to tell him they were almost there. Her breath caught as he smiled at her, the sun glinting off the sable locks of his hair, making them seem almost navy blue. His dark eyes were so filled with contentment. That was it. He looked *happy* in a way that he hadn't before today. Could it be that she had something to do with that? Maybe it was just that he'd shared the burden of his shame and guilt with someone else. Well, he seemed to like her at least. And find her attractive.

It was too much to hope that he was falling in love with her, Hope knew that. He was too brutalized by his past, too untrusting to open his heart to her. Yet knowing that didn't stop her wishing. For so long now she'd had gentlemen profess their undying love and devotion. None of it had ever stirred her, even a little. She'd thought that perhaps she'd been ruined by the heroes of her romantic novels. Thought that she'd made it impossible for a real gentleman to live up to those in her books.

But now, well, now she knew that she hadn't been interested because she hadn't loved them. Had barely even liked them. And the devotion they wrote sonnets and letters about…that wasn't real. They didn't love her because they didn't know her. They wanted a pretty wife for their arms and not much beyond that. They filled her home with flowers and her ears with platitudes, but it was all shallow, all disingenuous.

Gideon hadn't professed any sort of love. But he at least knew her, beyond her smile or her hair or her eyes. She was unapologetically herself with him, and he seemed to enjoy that. He listened when she talked and cared about what she said. And he'd trusted her with his awful, disastrous family secret. But did that amount to anything beyond this? Probably not. Even if he wasn't jaded, scarred from the past, he was leaving Halton soon and that would presumably be that.

The idea of him leaving forever made her feel unspeakably sad. *But today*, she told herself firmly, *was not a day for sadness*. She would have plenty of time to wallow in the misery of missing him when he was gone. In fact, she was starting to think that she would likely spend the rest of her life missing him.

Nobody had ever compared to him. She didn't think anyone ever would.

Firmly shutting out any and all unhappy thoughts of a lonely future, Hope turned to him with a smile pasted onto her face.

"Here we are," she declared.

He looked at the willow, its branches leaning down to kiss the surface of the lake.

"It's very pleasant," he said politely. "But…"

"Come on," she interrupted him, reaching out and plucking the blanket from his grasp. She knew that this special spot of hers didn't look like much. But once they stepped through the branches…

She heard his slight gasp and turned to grin triumphantly up at him.

As a girl, Hope and her sisters had stumbled upon this spot, and over the years, when the others had grown less interested in it, Hope had kept coming back. Hidden by the branches of the willow tree, a smooth, flat rock jutted out over the lake. Usually, the water was a bit too cool for her to swim in since the spot was permanently shaded. But to sit and read and think, was perfect. Even someone passing close by wouldn't see her sitting underneath the canopy of the willow. It was perfectly quiet, perfectly secluded, and big enough for two.

"So," she said casually. "Now that I've shared my secret hideaway with you, don't you think I deserve to be fed?"

Chapter Nineteen

THE SHADE OF the willow was a blissful reprieve from the baking midsummer sun, but Gideon still felt overheated.

It was likely more to do with the lady sprawled out on the blanket beside him than the weather.

After they'd eaten the simple repast of bread, cheese, and fruit tarts that Cook had provided, and drunk the lemonade, she'd made light work of ridding herself of the white redingote and then, to the detriment of his poor overworked heart, she reached down and removed first her boots, then her stockings.

He'd never known a woman so unconcerned with propriety. And he'd never been more grateful in his life.

Now, she lay back, her hair unbound, one arm tucked under her head, a look of utter contentment on her face.

"If you faint from overheating, I shan't be attempting to carry you back to the gig, just so you know," she said, her eyes still closed.

"What do you mean?" he asked, wondering if she knew how close he'd been watching her and how much it was affecting him.

She opened one eye, watching where he sat facing her, his back leaning against the trunk of the willow tree.

"I mean you must be too warm in all those layers. Why don't you remove some of them?"

She couldn't know how seductive, how risqué such words were. Couldn't know the immediate and deuced uncomfortable effect they had on him.

"Do you make a habit of trying to disrobe poor, innocent gentlemen in secluded spots, Miss Templeworth?"

She laughed, the sound deep and husky and painfully tempting.

"Of course." She grinned. "Why do you think I lured you here?"

Christ, she was a handful. But he couldn't remember a time he'd ever felt happier, more relaxed, *freer* as though the trials and tribulations of the last few years no longer had the power to ruin his life, or his relationship with his brother, or his future in the way that he'd once feared.

"Fine." He shrugged. "I suppose it's only fair since I've seen all of you." He winked.

He watched fascinated as her cheeks pinkened. How she could be so outrageous, so flirtatious, yet still easily brought to blush? Gideon had no idea but it was heart-achingly endearing.

"How ungentlemanly of you to bring it up," she groused.

Gideon merely quirked a brow as he reached up and began to unbutton his superfine. Her eyes tracked each movement of his hands, and his gaze tracked hers. Because he was watching her so closely, he saw her swallow as he shucked off the jacket, followed quickly by the grey waistcoat, then moved to untie his cravat.

"You're right," he said, his words almost guttural. "This is much better."

She sat up, her cheeks now a deep, flaming red.

"Good," she said tightly before clearing her throat once, twice, then swinging her legs around so her back was to him and her feet were dangling in the water. She hissed as her feet hit the lake. "Ugh, I forgot just how cold it gets." She shuddered but didn't remove her feet from where she lazily kicked them beneath the surface.

"You don't fancy another dip?" he asked, grinning wickedly as he took a seat beside her.

She turned her head, and her gaze dropped to his now bare

feet, the breeches he'd rolled up above the knee.

"It's far too cold here," she sniffed, averting her eyes.

Gideon didn't answer as he dipped his own feet in, but he couldn't contain his curse as his feet hit the icy water. "Damn it, that's freezing."

Hope's laugh rang out. "I did warn you."

"Yes, but I thought I'd impress you with my manliness in being able to handle it," he retorted, earning another laugh.

"You men." She shook her head. "Always looking for a way to show off."

"And how else are we supposed to gain the favor of fair ladies?"

"I didn't know you were trying to gain favor," she said with a saccharine smile. "I could have given you some advice."

"You are wicked, Hope Templeworth. Has anyone ever told you that?"

"Oh, yes." Her smile widened. "In fact, I consider it a slow day if at least three people don't point out how wicked I am."

Gideon's laughter came as easily as breathing.

"Your poor father," he said suddenly. "How on earth does he keep the reins on any of you?"

To Gideon's surprise, her smile dimmed, the light in her eyes banking.

"My father doesn't much bother with any of us," she said softly. "Not even Elodie."

Gideon couldn't have said why, but a surge of protective outrage whipped through him. What sort of man didn't care about his own daughters? If he had daughters, especially one as precious as the woman sitting beside him, he'd lay down his life for them.

"Then he's an idiot," he said simply, not caring if he was being insulting. However, he should have remembered to whom he was speaking.

"Indeed," she agreed easily. "He's idiotic for a great many things, not just his lackadaisical attitude toward his daughters.

That is the harsh truth. But no, I can't say that he much cares about any of us. In fact, none of us ever experienced the maddening overprotectiveness of the male of the species until Christian came along. Lord, but that man would have us all locked in towers if he could."

Gideon's respect for the other peer shot up at the words. He was glad, fiercely so, that someone cared enough to look out for the girls.

"I shouldn't think he'd manage to," he answered now, gently bumping her shoulder with his own. "I shudder to think what sort of escape plans you'd all hatch between you."

Her eyes gleamed with feral delight at his words. And he knew that they'd do it, too. They could be locked in a fifty-foot tower in the middle of the ocean and still manage to get out of it. They were a force of nature. Every last one of them.

"Well, we got Elodie out of Halton once and almost out of London, so I'm sure we could manage it."

"Almost out of London?" He was nearly afraid to ask, but curiosity got the better of him.

"Mm-hm. We were just about to get her on the stagecoach when Christian caught up and convinced her to marry him instead," she announced casually, as though it were the most ordinary thing in the world.

Gideon's stomach roiled a little at what could have happened to the viscountess if her madcap scheme had worked.

"Poor Lord Brentford," he said, shaking his head.

"Poor Christian? Why?" she asked. Well, demanded.

"Bad enough having to chase after the woman he loves, but to contend with an army of Templeworths? And then try to keep you all out of trouble. I think he could do with a hand, personally."

His words dropped like a stone into the air between them as he realized the potential ramifications of what he'd said. Brentford had, after all, only become responsible for the sisters by marrying one of them. And saying the man needed a hand, did she think he was volunteering somehow? *Was* he volunteering? The idea didn't fill him with fear, disgust, or panic. Only, only a sense of ...

"How dare you?" Her voice cut into Gideon's thoughts, filled with mock outrage. "My sisters and I are perfectly capable of running our own lives, thank you very much."

"Hmm," he said, pretending to consider her words, pushing his deep thoughts aside for the moment. "Precisely why you need sentries I should imagine. Sentries with access to a *lot* of brandy."

"You cad." She laughed, and before he knew what she was about, she kicked her leg toward him. He watched as the cool water hit him square in the face, soaking his hair and chest along with it.

He could only gape as she burst into peals of laughter.

"You don't think I'm going to let you away with that, do you?" he asked, dropping his voice to a menacing purr.

Her eyes widened, and she squealed as he reached out and dragged her onto his lap.

"Care for a swim, sweetheart?" he asked.

She twisted and wriggled against him as she pleaded and begged through breathless giggles, and he had to grit his teeth against the surge of desire that raged through him at the movement.

"This is my favorite gown," she protested, lifting a beseeching gaze to his face.

Gideon stilled as he gazed into the depthless brown pools of her eyes. He didn't believe the little liar for a second, but he was fast learning that he was no match for those eyes.

"How can I deny you anything when you look at me like that?" he asked wryly, reaching up to brush a lock of golden hair from her cheek.

Her laughter melted into a smile of such joy that it took Gideon's breath away, and he could do nothing but lean down to kiss her. He was a slave to her and to the feelings she evoked in him. And as he bent his head toward her own, he wondered if he should tell her that.

Chapter Twenty

THE FEEL OF Gideon's body pressed against her own set Hope's heart fluttering wildly even before he swept his tongue inside her mouth.

She'd known last night when she'd been in a similar position that he was strong and powerful and muscled in a way that made her breathless. But without his jacket and waistcoat, the heat of him seeped into her, and she found herself quite shockingly wishing that there were no barriers at all between his skin and her own. She wanted to feel all of him pressed against her. And the thought scared and delighted her in equal measure.

Pressing herself closer to the rigid length of him, Hope delighted in his growl against her lips. And then suddenly, she was moving. She gasped as he wrapped his hands around her waist and lifted her bodily from him. But before she could miss the contact, he'd laid her down on the smooth, flat rock beneath them.

And then, he was there, fitting himself against her so perfectly, so wantonly that she couldn't contain the moan that spilled from her mouth.

Gideon pulled his mouth from her own, moving to press kisses to her jaw, her neck, the pulse hammering at the bottom of her throat.

The water that she'd splashed on him dripped onto her neck, and her toes curled as his tongue darted out to lick the drop from her neck.

She thought it couldn't possibly get better. That was until he began to move. Hope couldn't keep still as his mouth moved from her neck, lower and lower. She arched her back in wild abandonment, and he took advantage of the movement to reach up and undo the ties at the back of her gown.

She should stop him, Hope knew. This was too much. They had made no declarations, no promises to each other.

But the feel of his lips was a pleasure she didn't have the strength to fight. He pulled at her loosened gown, and though she'd tried to talk some sense into herself, Hope found her shoulders moving to release the fabric, found herself impatiently waiting as he pulled the garment down her arms until there was only her chemise and stays.

"You're so beautiful," Gideon groaned as he brushed a possessive, trembling hand over the slope of her breasts and down, past where the dress now gathered at her waist and lower still until he was bunching and lifting her skirts.

A modicum of sense reared its head, and Hope reached out to stay his moving hand.

"Gideon, we cannot," she gasped, though even she could hear the need in her tone.

He leaned up and pressed a surprisingly tender kiss on her mouth.

"I won't ruin you, Hope," he said softly against her lips. "You deserve more than that. But let me touch you," he begged. "Let me taste you."

Her only answer was to deepen their kiss, letting him taste her capitulation. And then, Gideon set about doing exactly what he'd asked. Hope could only lie back and revel in the feelings he unleashed. Every stroke of his fingers in her heated core, every lick, and bite against her sensitive flesh was utter bliss.

She writhed under his ministrations, feeling herself race toward the explosion that she now knew would result in the most exquisite ecstasy, so acute it bordered on pain.

His mouth, which had been worshipping her breasts moved lower, and she was so caught up in the maelstrom of feelings he drew from her body that she couldn't guess at his intention. It was only at the first, hot feel of his tongue against her center that she realized, and her hips shot up.

"Gideon," she gasped, half scandalized, half-wild with need.

"It's all right, sweetheart," he said against her flesh, the vibration of his voice sending rippling waves of pleasure through her body. "You taste incredible."

Nothing had ever prepared Hope for what such words, such actions would do to her. But coherent thought was beyond her as he returned that clever, wicked mouth to her core once more and just like that, her pleasure broke on a tidal wave that she was happily swept away in.

The bliss he'd drawn from her body last night was nothing compared to the release that barreled through her now, and she could only hold on for dear life, gripping the strands of his hair in her fingers as she made her way through the storm of emotions.

Gideon guided her through it all, wringing every drop of pleasure from her flesh that he could. Only when she stilled, her breathing still labored, did he slowly work his way back up her body until he was leaning over her and grinning.

"You," he reached up and pushed a dampened curl from her brow, "are incredible."

And even though something so momentous had just happened, even though she knew that she'd crossed a line that she likely shouldn't have, Hope just felt so *happy* that she could only answer his grin with one of her own.

"Funny," she said past the lump in her throat, "I was going to say the same thing about you."

He leaned down to snort his answering laugh against her throat. But as he shifted against her, Hope felt the still very present evidence of his desire press against her hips. And though she felt thoroughly sated, the feel of him had her craving more. She rolled her hips experimentally, enjoying the hiss she drew from the lips still pressed against her.

Reaching up, she took his face in her hands and pulled it up so his eyes met her own.

And she knew that she shouldn't say what she was about to say. Do what she was about to do. Knew that though she'd only walked a fine line between flirtation and scandal, she'd never crossed it. Had never wanted to.

But this was Gideon. The man that somehow, somewhere along the way had captured her heart completely and utterly. She loved him. Whether or not she should. Whether or not he was willing or even capable of offering her love in return.

It was foolhardy. Wanton and reckless. Yet Hope could not bring herself to care as she stared into his face.

"Show me," she whispered. "Show me how to give you the pleasure you've given me."

The light that flared in the depths of his eyes was unholy, and it sent a skittering lance of lust skating along her veins.

"I won't ruin you," he repeated, though it sounded more like a plea than a promise. "I won't take you on a damned rock, Hope."

Her heart thudded painfully at the words. Did that mean that he planned to do it somewhere more comfortable? She could only wonder as to why the thought made her feel excited and not scared or even insulted.

Perhaps she was a wanton after all. But only with him. Only ever with him.

He sounded so tortured, so tormented that she could think of nothing else to do but lean up and press a kiss to his cheek, right by his ear.

Pressed against him like this, she could feel his heart thundering against hers, and it gave her the courage to speak again.

"Show me," she said more firmly, pouring everything she felt for him into her eyes and hoping that he would see the words she was still too scared to say.

He mumbled a black oath under his breath, but he took her

hand and guided it slowly down his body.

Hope was trembling as he pressed her hand against him, an agonized groan ripping from his mouth. But it wasn't fear that made her shiver. It wasn't fear that heated the blood in her veins.

"Show me," she said again.

⋙✕⋘

SHE WAS QUIET for the duration of their short ride back to her father's house, but then so was he. It wasn't an uncomfortable silence, far from it. It was filled with all the things he wasn't yet ready to say, but all the things he knew deep down that he'd been feeling for a while now.

Their afternoon at the lake had been the single best of his life. Even now his cock stirred at the memory of her hands, her mouth. Gideon couldn't stifle the oath that sprung to his lips. He was worse than a green lad in the first throes of passion, but he couldn't help it.

He'd known that there was a passion to Hope Templeworth the likes of which he'd never seen. But to have experienced it. To have her respond so beautifully to him, to learn every inch of her and to have her learn every inch of him—it was exquisite. She was a quick study, and he knew there would never be another who raised such feelings in him.

He looked over to see her watching him, and he couldn't keep the smile from his face. Something of what he was thinking must have shown, for her cheeks flushed in that way he loved.

Only minutes ago, she'd been screaming his name for the second time that day, but here she sat, demure and blushing. The paradox was intoxicating.

"Do you think Sophia will accost us the second we return?" he asked casually, more to put her at ease than anything else.

"Oh, undoubtedly," she said lightly, albeit a touch quietly.

They needed to have a serious talk. He knew it, and he was

sure she must know it, too. But he needed to get his thoughts in order, sort out his jumbled feelings before he could begin to confess them to her.

He still planned to return to his seat in a couple of weeks, having made commitments to his staff there that he couldn't break. But if he had his way, he wouldn't be returning alone. Or at the very least, he wouldn't be returning without an understanding between him and the beauty at his side.

The beauty who was now rolling her eyes, flicking her unbound hair over her shoulder.

A vision popped into his head. One so simple, so wonderful that it took his breath away. Hope with him, just like this, at his home, a home they would share together, the Claremont ruby on her finger.

And then, unbidden, the thought came; the ruby was on the finger of another woman. A woman who'd made off with the ring along with a host of other Claremont heirlooms. The memory of Elaine felt like a poison seeping into an otherwise perfect day. But much as he tried to push thoughts of her away, he couldn't seem to do it.

He needed to speak to Kit. He needed to face up to the past once and for all. Make his peace and be done with it. If not for his own sake, then for the sake of the woman beside him now. Perhaps she wouldn't wear the family ring, but it wasn't good enough for her anyway. He'd get her something better. Something more unique, more precious. Just like her.

But the thought was little comfort, and he knew that there would be no peace for him now. Once the memories seeped in, there was little other than the end of a brandy bottle that could help him forget.

The manor house came into view, and he noticed her shoulders stiffen slightly. For a moment, he panicked that she was regretting what had happened between them, that she didn't want him around.

But then she grimaced, and he followed her line of vision to see three distinct faces pressed against a window.

"They're like bloodhounds," she griped, more to herself than to him. "They're going to know the second I walk in that, well…"

His own mood was confusing and not exactly easy right then.

"Would you mind terribly if we postponed your visit for dinner? I just…" She huffed out a breath. "My sisters will behave infinitely worse if you are there. Not Elodie, but the other two most definitely."

He didn't bother pointing out that in the usual way of things people were on their *best* behavior when guests were around, not their worst. Because he knew enough about her sisters to know that she was right. And he knew that she must be reeling from their afternoon together because he most certainly was.

But he couldn't stand to see any worry or discomfort on her face, so he raised a mocking brow.

"Are you uninviting me for dinner?" he drawled. "How terribly insulting of you."

As he'd hoped, she laughed.

"I'm afraid I am," she said with faux contrition. "But I promise to convince my mother to extend a real invitation. And you won't even need to bring your horses."

He looked back toward the house and noticed that there was a face missing.

"It seems your sister might very well already be on the move," he said. "So perhaps I should take my leave now."

"You don't mind?" she asked softly, an odd vulnerability that he didn't expect from her stamped across her lovely face.

And, even though he knew they had an avid audience, he couldn't stop himself from reaching out and brushing his knuckles across her cheek.

"Hope," he said her name like a prayer, the words drawn from a place deep inside him. "What a fitting name. Nothing else, nobody else, has ever made me hope to live a better life. Hope to be a better man. Only you."

Her eyes became suspiciously glassy, and she opened her

mouth to say something, but the doors of the manor house were suddenly thrown open, and before he could blink, she was out of the gig and running toward the house.

He worried that he had perhaps said too much, but right before she closed the door, dragging a loudly complaining Sophia back inside by the scruff of her jacket, she turned to smile at him, and Gideon made his way home knowing that he'd be dreaming about that smile all night long.

Chapter Twenty-One

"CHESKA OWES ME three guineas. Don't let me forget to collect before we go home."

Hope looked up to see Elodie smiling triumphantly down at her.

"And why is that?" she asked, putting down the novel she hadn't been able to concentrate on.

"She said you'd snuck off to see Lord Claremont, and I said you'd snuck off to get away from Mama's questions."

Hope rolled her eyes, then complained loudly as Elodie pushed and squeezed her way onto the swing she was occupying.

Yesterday the return to the house had been exactly what she'd thought it would be. Brutal, incessant, and difficult in the extreme. She couldn't give her sisters the answers they'd demanded, not with Mama wailing about the missed opportunity of potentially having an earl to dinner, and Christian watching everything she said and did like a hawk.

At one point, she really did worry that Gideon's talk of a tower might actually come true. It was sweet, nice even, that Christian cared so much about them. But it was also mighty inconvenient when she had so much that she needed to keep a secret.

It wasn't until later that night, when the household was abed, that she finally got to talk about him. She didn't give away all her secrets, of course. In deference to Sophia's age, but also because it just didn't feel right. Even though she had always shared everything with her sisters, what had happened between her and Gideon, well, it was for them and them alone.

So, when a knock sounded on her door at the stroke of midnight, heralding the arrival of Francesca, who immediately sat cross-legged on Hope's bed, she merely waited a while, and then, there was Sophia. Not twenty minutes later came Elodie, looking so disheveled that Hope didn't bother asking if Christian was awake or asleep.

As soon as Elle had taken up her spot on the end of the now-crowded bed, the questions started and this time instead of shying away from answering, Hope felt free to wax lyrical about Gideon, skipping the parts that made her blush. Which was quite a lot when she got to talking about it.

Thankfully, her sisters had seemed relatively happy with her explanations and excepting a few good-natured, teasing comments, they were happy to leave her to her thoughts and dreams. All of which were, unsurprisingly, filled with Gideon.

Even now, when Elodie half squashed her to death, she couldn't really stop thinking about him.

"Mama is still going on about him, then?" she asked, though she already knew the answer would be yes.

"Of course," Elle exclaimed. "You should hear her now, be-moaning her lot in life. Apparently not sharing yesterday's roast pheasant means she'll never have an earl for a son-in-law. Christian pretends to be irritated by it but, secretly, I think he's a little put out that he's been bumped down a bit in her esteem."

Hope could only laugh as she imagined Christian in one of his sulks. Elodie was so very lucky. Though Hope had always been happy for her sister, she'd never really realized how fortunate both Elle and Christian were in their marriage. The love they had for each other was a thing of real beauty. Elodie deserved the world, and she had it in her choice of husband. Christian never made any secret of how much he adored his wife. And Hope didn't begrudge them their happiness. To love and be so loved.

To be secure in the knowledge that one's husband was so very besotted.

And she couldn't help but wonder if she would have that for herself one day. If Gideon would perhaps heal enough from Elaine's betrayal, and his father's, too, to open his heart to her.

"She's invited the lot of them to dinner, you know?" Elle was speaking again. "Lord Claremont, his brother, Mr. and Mrs. Bell. The whole family!"

Hope's heart sank to her toes.

She wanted to see Gideon, of course. And his brother was perfectly pleasant and even rather good company. For a vicar. But Mrs. Bell hated her. And she certainly wouldn't approve of her for her nephew.

And even though Gideon wasn't exactly the type to be swayed by an elderly aunt's opinion, she'd still rather not have the woman scowling at her across the dinner table.

"When are they coming?" she asked rather glumly.

"Tomorrow night," Elodie answered. "I managed to convince her to wait until at least then. Give her a chance to calm down a bit."

"And give me a chance to pick a marvelously inappropriate gown to see if this time I can actually get Mrs. Bell to faint clean away."

It was a testament to the changes in Elodie's life that instead of scolding Hope, she merely cackled, then took her arm and dragged her inside to help choose the said gown.

Love, Hope supposed, at least love when it was with the right person, would do that. Change someone utterly and completely. For she herself had gone from someone who couldn't think of quiet married life without almost dying of boredom to thinking that nothing in the world sounded quite so wonderful.

GIDEON KNEW THAT his eyes were on stalks as he watched Hope saunter into her family's drawing room. Knew because Kit's rueful laugh was accompanied by Brentford's menacing growl.

Yesterday, he'd racked his brain thinking of a plausible reason to come see her. But he'd come up short. Perhaps wisely, since he was making it painfully obvious just how besotted with Hope he'd become.

It had been good in any case that he'd stayed at his uncle's house for the day. Because it had given him the chance to truly think about what he wanted. And once he allowed himself to face all of his anxieties, all of his fears and doubts, he realized that they were nothing. Nothing at all compared to how he felt about the woman standing across the room from him now.

The ghost of Elaine had hovered too long over his life, over every decision he'd made since she'd betrayed Kit. Betrayed them all, really. And Gideon had truly thought himself broken by the experience. Truly believed that his guilt for his part in it, his disgust for what she'd done had tainted his view of marriage and love and women forever. But now he knew that he was simply waiting for the right woman. That falling in love would ease all of his misgivings.

He wasn't ruined by past mistakes. He'd just been waiting for Hope. For his salvation. And it was madness he knew to have fallen so hard, so fast. Who could meet Hope Templeworth and not fall hard and fast? So that's precisely what he'd done. Fallen deeply in love with his lady of the lake.

She looked up then, as though she heard his heart call out to her, and her smile was breathtaking. She looked angelic in white satin, brilliant white diamonds gleaming at her throat and ears. But he knew what devilment lay beneath the surface of purity. Knew how to bring it out in her. And base creature that he was, he could think of little other than finally making her his in every way possible.

He wanted to go to her now, to take her in his arms and tell her that he loved her. To beg her to be his and then hide them both away until he'd had his fill of her. Though he didn't think the latter part would ever be possible.

"I'd suggest closing your mouth, Claremont, or you're likely to begin drooling. And I can tell you, my mother-in-law is terribly fond of these Persian rugs."

Gideon snapped his eyes to Brentford, who was watching him with a mix of amusement and displeasure on his face. And he had to remind himself that he was glad the girls had a man to look out for them, since their own father was utterly useless. But it didn't quite stop his hackles rising.

"And you always conducted yourself in a gentlemanly way when you met the viscountess?" he countered.

For a moment, the viscount merely blinked at him before smiling, the expression not quite meeting his eyes.

"Not exactly, no," he answered with blunt honesty. "But then, I'd fallen in love with Elodie long before she became the viscountess. That probably explains it."

It was as carefully worded an interrogation as could be. And though there was no outright questioning, the implications were obvious.

Gideon knew he owed Hope the truth before anyone else. She deserved to hear that he loved her before anyone else. She deserved to have a say in what she told her family and how she told them.

But, well, Brentford cared about Hope. Cared about all of them. And Gideon couldn't very well hold that against the man. Not when he himself had grown alarmingly protective of not just Hope but her sisters, too.

If she agreed to marry him, he'd be in the same situation as the viscount was now. And he likely wouldn't be happy about a man salivating over either Francesca or Sophia in his presence.

And so, he looked the other man in the eyes and gave as much of an answer as he was willing to give before speaking to Hope.

"Yes, I'd imagine that is as good an explanation as any," he said frankly.

The viscount eyed him for another minute or two.

"Love does make us foolish, does it not?" he finally said carefully.

And Gideon couldn't stop his eyes from seeking her out as he answered. "Indeed, it does."

He couldn't help but feel like he'd passed some sort of test as Brentford reached out and clapped his shoulder before turning away and seeking out his wife.

Chapter Twenty-Two

"AND HOW ARE you settling in now, Mr. Bell?"

Mama was using her most sycophantic voice, but she was truly in her element. She'd sat the viscount and the earl across from each other and was in raptures every time she looked down the table at her esteemed guests.

Hope just knew that she was fit to burst and would be wandering around Halton for days bragging to anyone who'd listen about the lords in her life. She was insufferable enough about Christian. The addition of Gideon was going to make her worse.

Not that Hope was assuming Gideon would be a permanent fixture in their lives, of course. Wishing it didn't make it so.

All evening, every time she'd looked his way, he'd been watching her. Now, seated beside him as she was, his body seemed to brush against hers an inordinate number of times. A brush of a hand when he was picking up his fork. The press of his thigh as he leaned forward to speak to Christian. She was on the brink of expiring from it all, especially because every now and again she would catch that sandalwood and bergamot scent that was distinctly Gideon and oh so delicious.

And every time their eyes met, his had been filled with a tenderness that she didn't think she was imaging. Especially because Sophia had remarked about how disgusting it was to witness.

Now that she was sixteen, she'd been forced to attend the

dinner. And in a gown, no less. She'd borrowed one of Hope's. A sky-blue satin that looked remarkably well against her chestnut curls and bright blue eyes. But anyone who tried to tell her so got cursed at or a vulgar gesture, so they'd wisely stopped commenting on it. The saving grace, Hope supposed, was that Sophia behaved herself enough to take Mr. and Mrs. Bell's compliments without sounding like a sailor on leave.

Small mercies, indeed.

Kit was all politeness as he answered her mother's questions, and Hope felt a sudden rush of affection for the man. He was so kind, so good. Her heart twisted when she thought about what that awful woman, Elaine, had put him through. How she'd humiliated him as a means to an end. And how she'd tried to pull Gideon into her diabolical plans.

"What could that poor goose have done to earn such ire?"

Hope looked up to see Gideon grinning at her and realized that she'd trained her eyes on her dinner plate while she'd been thinking about his stepmother. Even thinking it made her feel slightly ill.

"Just wool-gathering." She shrugged.

"Clearly, whatever you're gathering isn't very pleasant," he answered softly.

"Not particularly, no," she admitted.

"Am I in trouble?"

She blinked in surprise at the question. "Of course not," she answered. "Why would you think that?"

"I suppose I'm just so used to being on the receiving end of that scowl. It's quite disconcerting that I've been replaced by a roasted bird."

Her burst of laughter earned her a disapproving scowl from both Mama and Mrs. Bell.

"Now look," she griped. "You've gotten *me* in trouble."

"Something I'm sure you're well used to," he parried dryly.

"Perhaps," Hope conceded, her heart racing at his wicked grin. "But your aunt already despises me, so let's not give her any more ammunition, hmm?"

She expected him to laugh, but he frowned, suddenly all seriousness.

"My aunt despises you?"

"You haven't noticed?" she asked, curious as to how upsetting he appeared to find the news. "Surely, she warned you about me?"

He looked thoughtful for a moment.

"Yes, perhaps she did," he answered slowly. And then, that grin swiftly returned. "Thankfully, I'm not all that concerned with my aunt's opinion. We'll just make sure to keep our distance."

It took a moment for his words to sink in, and when they did, Hope wasn't quite sure what to make of them.

"We, what?"

A footman arrived to clear their plates before Gideon could answer, and by the time they'd refilled wine glasses and served the next course, Papa, who had deigned to speak, was engaging Gideon in some boring conversation about the upcoming harvest season.

Hope could only pick at her food, her heart racing, butterflies dancing in her belly. Of course, it would not do to speculate and overthink what he'd said. One throwaway comment signified nothing. She knew that.

But trying to calm down by giving herself a stern talking-to wasn't working. And when his hand once again brushed against her own, causing her to drop her glass and spill claret all over Mama's table linens, she knew that nothing was likely to calm her.

Especially not when she could hear him laughing softly beside her.

"Miss Templeworth, it is such a beautiful evening, I wondered if you might take some air with me."

Hope had half a mind to deny Gideon's request as he made a beeline for her in the drawing room.

She was still tied in knots by his cryptic remark at dinner, and she'd had to endure endless, mindless gossip from Mama and Mrs. Bell, whilst they awaited the gentlemen's arrival after their port and cheroots.

But, of course, she wouldn't do that. Not least because she was simply dying to get to the bottom of what he'd meant when he'd mentioned "we." She wouldn't allow herself to guess, lest she get her hopes up, only to have them dashed.

The problem was that it was hard *not* to when he looked at her like that.

So, she pasted a polite smile on her face and took the hand he was holding out to her.

"I'd be delighted to, Lord Claremont," she simpered, and she knew that he knew she was putting on a show by the way he squeezed her hand and rolled his eyes slightly.

"What a nice idea," Christian piped up from across the room. "Why don't I, oof."

He was cut off suddenly by a none-too-subtle elbow to the ribs from Elodie, who winked conspiratorially at Hope. Thankfully, Mama didn't seem to notice, so entrenched was she in her coze with Mrs. Bell, and Papa had retired with the poor excuse of seeing to business matters.

Gideon jumped at the opportunity to escape that Elle had provided, and without another word to anyone, he swept out onto the veranda, dragging Hope in his wake. They came to a somewhat breathless halt as soon as they slipped outside, and Hope led the way to a darkened corner that she knew would be hidden from Christian's view, just in case Elle didn't manage to keep hold of him.

She fully expected Gideon to take her in his arms, smile, lean closer, and whisper sweet nothings in her ear. Her eyes drew closed in anticipation of just that.

"I hope your gown managed to avoid your clumsiness with the wine."

She snapped one eye open, then the other, to see him laughing softly.

"You, sir, are a knave and scoundrel," she grumbled. "My dress is fine, no thanks to you and your pawing at me over dinner."

"Mm, perhaps. But you only have yourself to blame. You shouldn't look so damned touchable."

Hope tried to rally herself to issue a scathing set down. She really would. Cheka would have chewed him up and spat him out for saying such a thing. But her brain seemed to have turned to the consistency of porridge around him.

"I'll keep that in mind for my next dinner," she quipped, albeit a little shakily. "Presumably, whomever I sit next to will be of the same mind."

The growl that accompanied the sudden glint of possessiveness in his eyes sent her poor, overworked heart hammering.

"It only counts," he said softly as he reached out and finally pulled her toward him, one hand spanning her waist, the other reaching up to cup her face, "when it's me you're next to."

"Is that so?" she asked, trying and failing to sound nonchalant. And the knowing quirk of his lips was proof that he knew how much he was affecting her.

Instead of answering, he bent his head and kissed her. His lips were soft but demanding, his body heated and solid against her own. Hope vaguely wondered if she'd ever get used to the tumultuous feelings he awoke in her, if she'd ever be able to control herself when he held her and touched and kissed her. It certainly didn't feel like it right now as her toes curled in her satin slippers, and her hands reached up to grab at his black dinner jacket and pull herself closer still.

His groan in response to the action elicited an answering one from Hope. Just like every other time, her control seemed to abandon her from the first contact between them, and she was already wondering if she'd manage to sneak him into her bedchamber when he began withdrawing from her.

"Luckily for both of us," he panted as he leaned his forehead against her own, and Hope was pleased that his breathing seemed as labored as her own. "I plan on being next to you quite a lot so we shouldn't run into any difficulties."

Just as his cryptic remark at dinner had sent a riot of butterflies loose in her stomach, so did his statement now. She dared not hope. He hadn't declared himself. Hadn't made any promises. Yet, what else could he mean? She was too scared to ask what she really wanted to, so she settled for the cowardly approach of hedging around it.

"A-aren't you leaving Halton soon?" she whispered.

His gaze seemed to bore into her very soul, and Hope found herself holding her breath as she awaited his answer.

"I am. But not alone. At least, I don't wish to return alone. Hope, I…"

"Gideon."

They both turned at the sound of a male voice calling out to see Kit standing in the open French doors, his face pale and grave. Hope tried to move out of Gideon's embrace, but he clamped his hand at her waist, refusing to allow her to budge.

And she stopped trying, focusing instead on calming the heart that was currently trying to burst out of her chest.

Had he been about to ask her to marry him? She didn't know, but oh, Lord how she wished it was so. She loved him so very much. The idea of being apart from him was something she simply couldn't get her head around.

She couldn't think of anything else he could have meant. And now he stood with her ensconced in his arms, he must know what such actions would look like.

Hope bit her lip to keep from grinning like an idiot. Especially because poor Kit looked as though he'd seen a ghost.

"Kit, what is it?" Gideon sounded vaguely annoyed as he

spoke to his brother. "I was in the middle of something rather important." Hope thrilled at the words. But his brother truly did look terrible. Perhaps he was unwell.

"Gideon," Kit spoke again, that one word filled with such dread that Hope's eyes widened in alarm.

Gideon obviously noticed his brother's despair, too, for his hand tightened on Hope's waist.

"She's back. She's here. Th-the servants told her where we were…"

"There you are."

Hope felt Gideon's entire body stiffen as a stunningly beautiful woman swept through the doors and onto the veranda.

"Gideon, aren't you going to say hello to your stepmother?"

Chapter Twenty-Three

GIDEON'S BODY FROZE as Elaine swept onto the veranda, smiling as though this were some sort of happy family reunion.

He watched as she brushed past Kit, who looked green around the gills, and came to stop in front of him. Her eyes, sharper and more cunning than ever before swept over Hope, and Gideon felt his jaw tighten.

He sidestepped as subtly as he could, putting himself between Hope and Elaine.

"I do apologize for ruining your little gathering." Elaine's voice was dripping with venom. "But it took me an age to track you both down and, well, I have some rather exciting news."

Gideon stifled a black oath as the veranda suddenly filled with Hope's family, and his aunt and uncle.

"Whatever it is, we can discuss it tomorrow. Leave your details with a servant on the way out, and we can arrange to meet."

He kept his tone icily calm but under the surface, his anger was venom in his veins. He had no idea what Elaine was up to, but it couldn't be anything good. He caught Kit's eye and saw that his brother was as worried as he was.

"That's no way to treat family," Elaine tutted. And Gideon wondered, not for the first time, if she might be genuinely insane. Because no rational person could act as she did, without conscience, without thought to others or the consequences of her actions.

"We are not family," he bit out, his tone freezing, his hands clenched to fists at his sides. Hope, who remained silent and watchful, reached out and brushed her fingers against his own. The gesture was fleeting but so comforting that Gideon felt his shoulders relax a little. A very little.

"Oh, but we are." There was something condescending in her tone that gave Gideon pause. And he knew, just knew that whatever was about to come out of her poisonous mouth was going to upheave his life. His only thought was to wonder if he could spare Hope from whatever was coming.

"I had thought to discuss this a little more privately but, well." She glanced over her shoulder at the gathering of his family and Hope's.

Kit still looked like he was going to be sick. Aunt and Uncle Bell looked concerned, which was touching. They knew the whole, sordid history of their entanglement with this woman. Mrs. Templeworth was positively agog. Even Mr. Templeworth looked vaguely interested.

Brentford was scowling, a simmering violence threatening in the viscount's eyes. And then, of course, there were Hope's sisters. Each of them with narrowed eyes pinned on Elaine.

"There's no particularly delicate way to put this, is there?" She laughed, and the sound gated against Gideon's already fraying nerves. "I thought the time had come for you to meet the latest member of the Claremont dynasty," she purred. "Though, he is of course not with me tonight. At such a late hour, the young viscount is fast asleep in bed. He is but two years old, after all."

The very air around the veranda stilled with the impact of Elaine's words. His father had been too ill to beget a child with the woman in front of her. And Kit had been far too morally conscious to anticipate his vows.

It couldn't be. It simply couldn't be. It was too awful to even contemplate.

But Elaine's viscously victorious smile was still firmly in place as she continued hammering the nail in.

"Congratulations, Gideon, darling. You have a son."

"So, this is where you're hiding?"

"I'm not hiding, I'm right here," Hope argued, trying to ignore the gleam of speculation in Elodie's eyes, so like her own.

Of course, one of her sisters would know to look for her here, at the willow tree. Her spot was now tainted with memories of Gideon and what they'd done here.

She stayed mutinously quiet under her sister's scrutiny, refusing to be the one to break the silence.

Elodie sighed and sat on the rock beside her before she reached out to grip Hope's hand.

"You love him, then."

Hope felt her mouth drop open at Elodie's frank words.

"What?" she spluttered, her laugh bordering on hysterical to her own ears. "You don't mean, I haven't…"

She was all set to deny it until she caught the understanding in Elodie's eyes and quite unexpectedly, she felt tears begin to form in her own. She had withstood Christian's suspicions, Mama's caterwauling, Cheska's inquisition, and Sophia's loud theatrics after her world had imploded quite spectacularly on that balcony last night. But it seemed she couldn't withstand the sympathy from her sister.

Elodie reached out and pulled Hope into a hug that she hadn't even known she needed, and she dropped her head onto her big sister's shoulder, just like she'd done as a child when something had upset her.

"How did you know?"

"Oh, that was easy. You look precisely as miserable as I did when I fell in love with Christian," Elodie said, pressing a kiss to her head.

"But Christian loved you back," she said miserably.

"Yes, well, if you'll remember he did a very good job of acting quite the opposite," Elodie said ruefully, and even Hope raised a tiny smile at the memory of Christian and that nasty business with his former mistress that had almost ended things between him and Elodie.

Hope had never seen a man so desolate as Christian the night he'd thought he was losing Elle forever. Thankfully, it had all worked out in the end. And it had only taken two almost kidnappings for them to sort out their problems and feelings for each other.

Sadly, she and Gideon stood no chance of having the same sort of ending. He had a child. A child with the woman who'd cuckolded his brother and then married his father! It sounded like the plot of a particularly nauseating tragic play. And Hope had known as she'd fled to her rooms last night and locked the door behind her that she didn't have it in her to be one of the players.

It wasn't until this morning when she'd come downstairs to break her fast and face the music, as it were, that she even found out what had happened last night. Her unusually subdued sisters had explained how Gideon's first instinct had been to chase after her. And how that instinct had resulted in a tense standoff between him and Christian.

It had only been when Cheska had threatened to throw the unwelcome dowager countess off the balcony that Gideon had seen fit to get her out of there. They all warned her, however, that Gideon had looked like a man possessed and was likely to come hammering the door down any second.

So, Hope had run. Coward that she was, she'd just gotten up and left the table, the house. The grounds even. Coming here probably hadn't been her brightest idea, given that Gideon knew what it meant to her. But her feet had brought her here without her even thinking much about it.

Her heart still ached as much as it had last night. She'd been so close to getting everything she'd ever wanted. She'd been so sure that Gideon was about to declare himself. Now she didn't know how she felt. How Gideon felt. What the consequences of all this were.

He had a *son*. A son with the woman who'd married his father. It was more than she could stand.

"My offer still holds, you know. Just point me in the direction of a balcony."

Hope lifted her head from Elodie's shoulder, wiping at her eyes as Cheska and Sophia marched through the curtain of willow branches.

"If I decide the best course of action is murder, you'll be the first to know." She laughed. But the sound was as pathetic as any she'd ever made.

"It's quite disgusting, really, isn't it?" Sophia threw herself on the grass and leaned against the trunk of the tree as Elle and Hope turned to face them. Cheska sat beside Sophia in a flurry of periwinkle skirts. "I don't think the Bard himself could have come up with such a tragic family setup."

"It's not Gideon's fault, though." Hope immediately jumped to his defense.

"Isn't it?" Francesca asked with her usual brutal honesty. "Last I checked, it required a certain amount of participation on a man's part to impregnate a woman."

Hope rubbed at her aching temples. She'd had a headache all morning. Likely because she hadn't slept a wink the night before. Or maybe a headache was a symptom of a broken heart. She wouldn't know, since this was the first, and hopefully the only time, she'd ever experience such a thing.

She wanted to defend him further, but she couldn't do so without explaining the whole, sordid tale, and she didn't want to break Gideon's confidence like that. It wasn't her story to tell.

"It's complicated," she said weakly. "There are extenuating circumstances."

"So, he didn't tup his stepmother?" Cheska blurted.

"Cheska!"

Elodie's admonishment fell on deaf ears, as she must have known it was.

"She wasn't, ugh. Yes, they had a—uh—entanglement," Hope tried to explain. "But it was before she married his father." They all shuddered at that, and Hope truly didn't blame them. "He didn't know who she was, but she knew who he was, and she tried to trick him. When it didn't work, she moved on to the earl."

She looked at the faces of her sisters, each wearing masks of varying degrees of sympathy. For her or Gideon, Hope couldn't have said.

"It's just a mess," she finished quietly.

Nobody spoke for a while, and then Francesca, who'd been staring out at the lake, a contemplative look on her face, turned to face Hope.

"If she is capable of sinking to such lows, is Claremont even sure that the child is his?"

"No, I'm not."

They all whipped around at the distinct sound of Gideon's voice behind them. Hope's breath caught as she raked her gaze over him while she slowly stood. He looked as bad as she felt. His hair was disheveled as though he'd been raking his fingers through it, and he obviously hadn't shaved since yesterday since his jaw was shadowed with dark stubble.

It was grossly unfair that it only managed to make him more handsome, more mysterious and menacing looking.

"He looks like a pirate," Sophia whispered loudly enough to wake the dead, and Hope rolled her eyes.

"He does," Cheska said. But there was an appreciation in her tone that set Hope's teeth on edge. "All dark and brooding. It suits him."

Usually, Gideon would have found her sister's outlandish comments amusing, Hope knew. Perhaps he would have been a bit arrogant about it. But he didn't even glance in their direction. His eyes, desolate and bleak, remained fixed on her and only her.

"I need to talk to you," he said, taking a step toward her. Just one step before he came up against a wall of Templeworths. Hope almost smiled as she remembered a similar situation where she, Cheska, and Sophia had shielded Elodie from Christian. They were, after all, each other's fiercest supporters, and she was never more grateful to them.

But she needed to hear whatever Gideon had to say. If only so that she could say goodbye and walk away if she needed to.

"It's fine," she told her sisters. But not one of them budged.

Gideon's lips quirked ever so slightly.

"I brought my stallion," he said to Sophia. "He's tied up just behind us."

It was exactly the right thing to say, for Sophia immediately broke rank and ran in the direction of the horse. Only Elodie wordlessly reaching out to grab at the back of her riding jacket stopped her.

"Nice try," Elodie said with more bite than Hope had ever heard before.

"Please," Gideon spoke over their heads directly to Hope, and there was a world of agony in his voice. So much so that her bruised and broken heart melted.

"I want to talk to him," she said more firmly to her sisters. They turned to look at her and after a while, Elodie nodded briefly.

"Come along," she said to the other two, and miracle of miracles, they actually listened.

Sophia shot off in the direction of the horse with Elodie swiftly moving after her, throwing a small, encouraging smile in Gideon's direction.

Francesca brought up the rear, but she paused beside Gideon and ran a look over him.

"How do you feel about the murder of family members?" she asked casually as though asking if he was enjoying the weather.

To his credit, Gideon only blinked a couple of times before answering.

"I'd say depending on the family member, I'm in favor of it," he answered roughly.

Francesca raised a brow and gave him a terrifyingly innocent smile.

"That was the right answer," she drawled before sauntering after her sisters.

Chapter Twenty-Four

GIDEON'S HEART HAMMERED relentlessly. He truly thought that if he could survive Hope's sisters, he could survive anything. But looking at the unbearable sadness in her beautiful eyes, well that wasn't something he could endure. "I'm sorry, Hope. I'm so sorry that you had to see that. That your family had to see that."

The words he'd been holding in since she'd run from him last night spilled out of him. He hadn't slept, he hadn't spoken a word to Kit or his aunt and uncle. He hadn't even begun to process what Elaine had told him and what the potential ramifications were. Because he hadn't been able to think of anything beyond Hope. Beyond how she must be feeling and what he needed to do to make sure this didn't destroy everything between them.

"You don't need to be sorry," she mumbled. "You didn't ..." She swallowed, and he hated how hesitant she seemed, how small. His brave, beautiful Hope timid and meek because of him and his damned past mistakes.

But if it was true, if he really was a father, how could he ever think that anything other than a blessing? Christ, it was such a colossal mess. One he was still reeling from; one he couldn't even begin to process. And as far as he was concerned, there were only three innocent people who didn't deserve to get caught up in it. Kit, Hope, and that little boy.

His own feelings were secondary to all of that. He'd only

spoken again to Elaine after he'd removed her from Hope's home last night to find out where she was staying before he'd had to walk away from her. And then he'd sent Kit and his aunt and uncle home in his carriage, needing to be alone. Needing to walk off some of the roiling emotions he was drowning in.

But he hadn't been able to concentrate, to even begin to sort out his thoughts and feelings. All he could think of was Hope. The shock and confusion she must be feeling. And underneath it all, the fear. The fear that even now had him terrified that he'd say the wrong thing or make the wrong move.

What if this was too much for her? He'd wanted to make her his wife, the mother of his children. He'd wanted to build his life around her, for her. Now he didn't even know if he'd get the chance to.

She heaved a sigh and looked up at him, he could see from the redness around her eyes that she'd been crying, and his heart cracked at the sight.

"What does this mean?" she whispered, the words fractured, her voice raspy.

He wanted to tell her that it didn't mean anything. That it didn't change anything. But how could he? The last thing he wanted was to drag her into such an ugly situation. She deserved only happiness. She deserved to have someone with a clean slate. Someone who could give her the whole world. The moon and stars if she asked for them.

He could tell her that he loved her but that wasn't fair, was it? Not now. It would be unpardonably selfish. Just as it was unpardonably selfish to want her so damned much. To lean on her and share these burdens with her.

He couldn't do it. He wouldn't.

"I don't know," he said softly. "There is so much I need to look into. So much I need to try to understand."

"But he's here? Your son?"

He flinched slightly, unable to help himself. Could it really be that he had a son? It didn't feel real to him. It didn't feel *right*. And he knew that probably made him a bastard in a way he'd never allow a child of his to be one.

And that, that was what it came down to, wasn't it? If he had a son, he *had* to do whatever it took to do right by him. Even if it meant letting go of the woman who owned his heart. The only person he'd ever felt true happiness with.

"Elaine is staying in an inn outside Halton." He didn't miss how she winced at the name. "I don't know anything beyond the fact that she's decided to stay in England. For now, at least."

"With your son."

The ramifications weren't lost on either of them. He wasn't just a man—he was a peer of the realm. And he was expected to put title and duty before everything else. Even if that meant acknowledging the boy to save the family from scandal. And the only way to do that was to marry the child's mother. The boy was still young enough that by the time he was at the age to go to school, the ton would have moved on from any whiff of scandal around his name. Or pay Elaine enough to get rid of them both. And what sort of blackguard would that make Gideon? To father a child and then abandon him because his presence was an inconvenience?

"I take it she's not going to pretend that he's your father's child?"

"Who would believe that he was?" Gideon countered miserably. "Besides, if he is mine," he tripped over the words, loathe to say anything that would hurt her more, "Then he deserves everything that comes with that. He deserves to be acknowledged."

She only stared at him, and for the first time since he'd set eyes on his lady of the lake, he saw nothing in her expression. Not pain. Not sorrow. Not even anger. Just nothing. And that was perhaps worse than anything else.

"This isn't what I wanted for you. For us." She must know that, but he had to say it anyway. Had to get it out. "Last night, you have to know before Elaine arrived, I…"

"Don't." The word was short, emotionless. And as he stared at her, his heart feeling as though it were cleaving in two, Gideon couldn't help but feel like this might be the last conversation she would ever allow him to have with her.

SHE COULDN'T BEAR it, Hope thought frantically. She couldn't stand here and listen to him say that he was sorry and then leave her behind anyway. It was too much.

"I know how hard this must be for you," Gideon said. "I cannot imagine how you're feeling right now."

"I don't need your sympathy, Gideon," she snapped, unable to keep the sharpness from her tone. But she was on the verge of losing what little control she had over herself. It wouldn't be fair to either of them when no amount of crying would change the situation they found themselves in.

And she wouldn't have him feel the need to apologize for the birth of an innocent babe. She knew from their talks that his own father had been cold and unfeeling. And that's not who he would want to be.

"Then what do you need?" The desperation in his tone almost broke her. "Tell me, and I swear to you, if it's in my power to do it, I will."

Hope's heart splintered at the agonized sincerity in his words.

He had no idea, no idea at all that it *was* in his power to give her what she needed. Because it was him. His heart, his soul, every part of him was what every part of her needed. Because she already belonged to him. Wholly and completely.

But she wouldn't tell him so. Wouldn't be so cruel as to subject him to the same anguish she was currently feeling. Not when she knew it wouldn't change anything.

"I think," she said past the lump in her throat, "that you should concentrate on navigating your way through whatever this is. And I don't think Halton is the place in which to do it."

Her heart squeezed so tightly that she could barely get the words out.

"Hope," his whisper was devastated and devastating.

"We both know that you need to figure this out, Gideon," she said, pushing down every feeling, every emotion. Burying them so deep that she knew her voice had lost inflection completely. "I hope that you will be happy. I sincerely wish you the best with whatever path you end up taking."

"Don't do this." His words were a storm of emotion in comparison to her own flat tone. And she couldn't stand it. It was too hard not to throw herself into his arms. Beg him to stay with her and say to hell with everything else. But she could never ask it of him, and she wouldn't in any case. He wasn't the type of man to shirk his responsibilities, and she wouldn't love him so much if he were.

"I have to go," she mumbled as she tried to hurry by him.

His touch was a brand against her cool skin.

"Hope, I lo…"

"Don't," she interrupted as agony swept through her. She could guess as to what he would tell her. And just yesterday the words would have been the most beautiful thing in the world. But now? Now they would just hurt. "Please don't. I can't bear it."

He stared at her, looking into her very soul, his eyes growing glassier with every second.

But finally, he let her go.

"I'll come back," he said firmly, his tone brooking no argument. "I won't say or do anything until I know I'm in a position to make you happy, to give you the life you deserve. But I'll come back, Hope. For you. For us."

Every word cut her a little bit deeper.

"Whatever it takes, however I can, I will find a way to make this right. I swear it."

There was so much she wanted to say and so much that she

couldn't. Hope did the only thing that felt right. She reached up and pressed her lips against his, putting everything she felt but could not speak into the action. And when she made to pull away, when his hands reached up to stop her, to hold her face and deepen the kiss, she let it happen, knowing that she would have only this to cling to for however long it took him to keep his promise and return.

Finally, when she thought her lungs might explode, he released her and allowed them both to draw breath. There were no words left. None beyond what would make things so much more complicated if either of them dared to utter them now.

And so, she simply stepped back, turned, and walked away, feeling his eyes on her until she was out of sight.

Chapter Twenty-Five

G IDEON COULD HAVE wept with relief as he spotted the candlelight flickering in the window of the farmhouse where he and Kit now arrived.

For three weeks he'd been on the road. Not at home where he should have been. Not in Halton where he wanted to be. But on this damned wild goose chase through the English countryside.

He had no idea what exactly Elaine was up to, but he was determined to find out once and for all.

Even now, the memory of that last meeting with Hope haunted him.

Though the weather had turned dramatically cooler and wetter, it was almost impossible to see anything through the dark, driving rain since she still lingered in his mind. Her taste, her scent, the feel of her pressed against him. Even the color of her eyes and that wicked curve of her lips. Every part of her stalked every second of his day.

He just wanted her back. From the moment he'd left Halton, he'd missed her. And though he'd had plenty to occupy his time, the craving for her hadn't eased.

"Do you think we've finally managed to track her down?"

Gideon turned toward Kit, who was just as soaked as he was atop his own mount. "Let's hope so," was his only answer. He was tired, cold, miserable, and furious that this woman had swept into his life once more, destroyed what little peace and happiness he had, and then run away again.

The day after his heartbreaking goodbye with Hope, he'd arrived at the inn she'd been staying at, only to be told that she'd left. Yes, she'd had a young boy with her and no, they hadn't left alone. A gentleman, though the innkeeper had used the term lightly, had arrived the night before, Gideon was informed. And by early the next morning, the dowager countess was gone, leaving behind a hefty bill.

Gideon had paid the man on his way out the door and thus had begun three weeks of following the trail of tidbits of information. Every inn he and Kit had come to had told the same tale. The dowager countess, a babe, and a man racking up bills that they left without paying. And Gideon had settled every one of them.

The only bit of luck they'd had was when the busybody wife of the last inn they'd stopped at had told them about how she'd proudly eavesdropped on their conversations and had found out that the mysterious gentleman owned a farmhouse, not ten miles from the town they were currently in. And that they'd talked staying there for an indeterminate length of time and for an unknown reason.

So now, here they were. Gideon had no idea what Elaine was playing at, but he knew it couldn't be anything good. Still, at least they appeared to have tracked her down, and if nothing else, he could at least get plans in place to get back to Hope.

As usual, as soon as he thought of her name, his heart twisted painfully. If he lived a thousand years, he'd never forgive himself for even inadvertently causing Hope pain.

"Come," Kit said gently as though he could guess the direction of Gideon's thoughts. "The sooner we get this over with, the sooner we can get back to Halton."

Gideon nodded his agreement, then kicked his exhausted horse into movement. Not for the first time, he wished that he'd taken the time to arrange for his carriage to be made available before he'd set out on this tedious journey. But his shock and confusion had been so intense, his pain at leaving Hope so raw, that he hadn't been thinking straight. Only Kit accompanying him had made him even stop for food and rest that first night.

They rode around the side of the house, guessing that they could stable the horses there. Indeed, they found a dilapidated stable that had clearly fallen into disuse some time ago. But the roof was solid and there was fresh hay, if not much of it, along with a carriage that had seen much better days, and a pair of aging mares.

The brothers only took the time to unsaddle the horses and dig out some oats and hay before making their way to the back of the farmhouse. "Do try to keep your cool, Gideon," Kit cautioned him as he banged on the door.

The front would have been politer, but something told Gideon not to give too much warning that he was here. That he'd found her.

The door creaked open, and Gideon looked down into the unwashed face of a man clearly in his cups.

"Who the hell are you?" the man slurred, and even from outside, Gideon could smell the alcohol and stale sweat on the creature.

"I'm looking for Lady Claremont," he said as evenly as he could. "And the boy she has with her."

The man scowled up at him suspiciously, swaying slightly on his feet.

"The who?"

"Elaine," Gideon gritted.

"What do you want with her?"

Though he wasn't dressed like a gentleman, whoever this was he'd clearly been Quality at some point in his life if his cultured, clipped tone was anything to go by.

"Darling, why do you have the door open?"

At the sound of Elaine's voice behind the drunkard, Gideon slammed his weight into the rickety door and stepped inside the drafty kitchen, Kit on his heels. He quickly took in his surroundings, cracked, peeling paint, furniture that had seen better days, a meager fire burning in a sooty hearth. And there in the middle of the room, with a young boy on her hip, was Elaine.

Her eyes widened as she stared at Gideon's glowering features, but his focus was on the boy. The bright blonde hair and distinctive green eyes. Nothing like Gideon's, but very much like the man's now standing behind him.

"What the bloody hell is going on?" the stranger demanded.

Gideon kept his gaze on Elaine as he answered. "An excellent question," he drawled sarcastically, the quiet tone belying the volcanic rage bubbling inside him. He began to suspect that he'd been the target of a scheme that had, for some reason, gone awry. "Why don't we let my stepmother explain? Because I sure as hell would like to hear it."

TWO HOURS LATER, Gideon's head was pounding, and he'd heard nothing from either Elaine or her paramour to cool his temper. Kit, ever the peacemaker, had convinced them all to sit down and get to the bottom of whatever the hell was going on.

He'd suggested tea, but there was none to be had, so they were nursing cheap rum in chipped porcelain tankards.

He wasn't a father. She hadn't borne him a child. He was free. No ties to the mercenary creature scowling at him now. Gideon hadn't been able to tear his eyes from the boy. The boy who was the very picture of Elaine's lover. Charles Pearce, a once-wealthy gentleman who'd gambled away all his assets and money and then, apparently, moved on to Elaine's.

For her own part, Elaine had sobbed and wailed and begged for understanding and then shamelessly for money. Not at first, of course. At first, she'd tried to brazen it out by insisting that the boy, also named Charles, was Gideon's and that he needed to recognize him as his son and provide for them both.

When it was obvious that her drunken lover had forgotten whatever role he was supposed to play and had gone on and on about how he was going to win enough money to give his boy a gilded life, she'd had no choice but to come clean.

Charles, it seemed, was supposed to have stayed here undetected until Elaine got her hands on some funds. Apparently, the generous monthly stipend she received wasn't enough to feed and clothe them all, as well as provide for Charles's gambling addiction. Once she'd tricked Gideon either into marrying her to do right by his 'son', or paid her off to stay quiet, she would send for her gambler and they'd live in drunken bliss on Gideon's money, with him holed up somewhere nearby. It was beyond distasteful. Beyond ridiculous, too.

When the idiot, who had by now drunk himself into a stupor and passed out on the floor like a dog, had shown up in Halton, Elaine had panicked and run with him. And now, here they were. Her son, who was a lot younger than she'd implied when she'd tried to use him so ill, was asleep in her arms, and Gideon stared at him now, his feelings as riotous as ever before.

He had to admit to being fiercely relieved that he needed no further contact with Elaine. Fiercely happy that he could go back to Hope, just as he'd promised. But that innocent babe, what sort of life would he have with these two idiots? He looked over to see Kit also staring at the baby, no doubt thinking along similar lines.

"You owe him more than this, Elaine," Gideon said when he could trust himself to speak without wanting to kill her.

He thought briefly of Francesca's threat, and for the first time in weeks, he managed a smile. A tiny one, but a smile, nonetheless.

It was gradually sinking in. He was free. Free to return to Halton and throw himself at Hope's mercy. Free to tell her how much he loved her, how he wanted nothing more than to be her husband and spend every day for the rest of their lives making up for any hurt these past few weeks had caused her.

Elaine glared at him, the fury in her eyes enough to bring his focus back to the task at hand. But lurking beneath the anger there was something like shame.

"Do you think I don't know that?" she hissed. "Why do you think I tried to get you to take care of him?"

"Grow up," Gideon lashed out. "And take care of him yourself. Stop trying to use me as a means to an end. What the hell is wrong with you?"

She tipped her chin up at his words, but he saw the small movement of her hands adjusting the boy's blanket, the finger she stroked along his chin. And perhaps he was going soft, perhaps loving Hope had simply melted away his natural cynicism, but he felt some of his anger cool.

"I don't know what made you like this, Elaine," he said softly but firmly. "And I don't particularly care. Before I met Hope, I would have said that it was simply your beauty that led you down a path of thinking your looks were your only value."

She flinched slightly, and he knew that he must be somewhat close to the mark.

"But if someone who looks like Hope Templeworth can find a way not to have her beauty define who she is, then you certainly can. And you damn well should, for his sake if nothing else." He nodded toward the babe.

"You have no idea what it's like," she snapped. "To be a female with little options."

"And neither do you," he countered, refusing to let her paint herself as some sort of innocent. "You used my brother ill when you could have had a good man, a decent man. And then you manipulated your way into being a damned countess. It's nobody's fault but your own that you threw away those opportunities. But I will tell you this, I know what it's like to grow up with a cold, unfeeling father. And no child deserves that fate."

Her eyes rounded, and she looked down at her son.

"There's no denying you love him," Gideon continued. "As

much as someone like you is capable of love in any case. But if you do not get yourself on a good, honest path, you are condemning him to a life of misery."

"How?" she whispered.

Gideon sighed. All he wanted was to get up, get the hell away from this woman who had caused him no end of heartache, and get back to his Hope.

"Marry that idiot so your son at least has married parents. Move somewhere new where people don't need to know he was born on the wrong side of the blanket. And hope that drunken lout drinks himself to an early death," he answered bluntly.

"Ah, perhaps there are other ways to help you plan a future for your boy," Kit, ever the kind soul, interjected. "The stipend is generous enough to give you and Charles a comfortable life, as long as you stop funding Mr. Pearce's gambling habits. And stop gambling yourself."

"But w-we have nowhere to go. I sold the house and the-the money is gone," she admitted, but at least she had the grace to look shamefaced about it.

Kit turned a beseeching look on Gideon, who rolled his eyes in response.

But…

Hope truly had made him soft, he decided as he found himself leaning forward, clasping his hands together on the scratched surface of the table.

"Who owns this place?" he asked.

"Charles won it in a card game years ago," she ran a faintly disgusted eye over her surroundings. A far cry from Claremont Park indeed. "But I don't want Charlie here, he does deserve better, you're right."

"I'm willing to give you one more chance, Elaine," he said against his better judgment. "One chance to get out of my life and stay out of it. I'll buy you a cottage. Something clean and well built," he said, running his own critical gaze over the ramshackle farmhouse. "In return, you will marry that boy's father. When he's old enough to be sent to school, I'll fund his education."

Her eyes widened, and even he could acknowledge the appreciation in them.

"I will keep an eye on him. You can write to me about his progress, but I don't want you anywhere near me or Kit. And especially Hope. If I find out you are not doing right by your boy, I'll cut you off. And I'll find a way to reduce your stipend, too."

Kit was gaping at him, the blackguard who'd sired her son snoring in the background.

"But I warn you," Gideon continued softly. "If I cannot undo the damage you've done to my relationship with Hope, I'll make you wish you were never born, Elaine. Do we understand each other?"

She had the good sense to nod her agreement.

Gideon got to his feet, and Kit followed suit.

"Stay here until I've found a suitable property," he instructed her. "I take it you haven't had access to your stipend since you've been on your travels?" He couldn't quite keep the disdain from his voice, though he didn't particularly care.

"No, I haven't."

He reached into his pocket and pulled out some banknotes, placing them on the table between them.

"You can write and tell them to send your money here for now. I'll have a house for you by the winter. Keep that money out of his clutches." He nodded toward the snoring heap of flesh in the corner.

"Thank you, Gideon."

It was the only time he'd ever heard her sound humble and sincere. But he didn't care. She meant less than nothing to him.

"I'm not doing it for you," he told her brutally, his eyes on the boy in her arms. "As far as I'm concerned, we're done. My man of business will be in touch."

Without another word, he walked out feeling a weight off his shoulders for the first time in weeks.

Chapter Twenty-Six

"MISS HOPE, IF it's possible, you get more beautiful every time I see you."

Hope gritted her teeth, biting back the sarcastic answer at the tip of her tongue. It wasn't Alphonsus's fault that she was utterly miserable and that every compliment she received now was jarring to her ears and sent a lance of pain through her heart.

She'd known the young man since they'd been children, and she really was trying to listen to his tales from the Continent about his Grand Tour.

"And I told our guide in Rome that even Helen of Troy herself could not have compared to our own Miss Templeworth. I was only sorry that I did not have a miniature to prove the truth to him."

"Oh, you're too kind, Alphonsus, but I think comparing me to Helen of Troy might be doing it a bit brown."

"No, indeed Miss Templeworth. I defy anyone to find any beauty in history or literature that could compare to yours. In fact, if I might be so bold, we were sailing on the Seine when I was inspired to write a sonnet in your honor."

"How lovely." She smiled weakly.

"I happen to have it on me now," he exclaimed to her horror and began patting at his jacket. "I just, ah yes. Here it is."

"Oh, I don't think…"

"No need to thank me," he simpered, and she had to grit her

teeth again.

She never should have allowed her siblings to talk her into attending tonight. For the past few weeks, since Gideon had left, she'd been more than happy to hide away at home and wallow in self-pity.

But they'd convinced her, and so she'd tossed on a rose-pink silk gown, the darker color in deference to the arrival of autumn, and now here she was with poetry being read at her in the middle of the magistrate's drawing room.

She cast a glance around for help, but none was forthcoming.

Sophia was being led through the steps of a cotillion, looking instead like she was being led to the gallows.

Cheska was throwing back a glass of champagne and ignoring the men attempting to engage her in conversation. And Elodie was, unsurprisingly, ensconced in a cozy little bubble with Christian, both of them still a little misty-eyed as they held hands over her stomach.

It had been the only bright spot in Hope's life since Gideon had left, when Elodie had announced that she was with child. Hope had burst into tears, which had surprised them all, including herself. She was happy for Elle and Christian of course. And so *excited* about having a niece or nephew to spoil. But the announcement had made her miss Gideon even more viciously than usual. And it had reminded her that, for all she knew, he was off somewhere with his ex-stepmother and doting over a child of his own.

But she'd refused to ruin Elodie's happiness with her own problems, so she'd shoved aside everything but the greatest happiness for her sister and thrown herself into chatter about the babe. Even Sophia had mustered up some excitement, promising that she'd have her niece—there was no doubt in Sophia's mind that it would be girl—in a saddle before she was out of leading strings.

Cheska had congratulated them heartily and then, because there was a distinct dearth of male company for Christian, had drunk brandy and smoked cigars with him until she'd thrown up.

All in all, it had been quite the celebration, and Hope had wished Gideon was there to share it so much that it was a physical ache. Heartbreak, she'd decided later that night when she'd been lying alone and just *missing* him, truly was powerful enough to kill a person.

"An Ode to Hope."

Alphonsus's booming voice cut into her thoughts, and she nearly jumped out of her skin.

"Really, Alphonsus you are very kind but perhaps…"

"Her hair is like the finest silk, the halo of a goddess."

"Alphonsus, please."

"Her eyes are pools of ethereal light, and yet she is so modest."

Well, now she was embarrassed because it was just plain bad.

"Her smile dazzles like sunlight, a work of finest art."

Hope looked around to see that they'd gathered something of an audience. An audience that included three cackling sisters and one chuckling brother-in-law.

Where was that overprotective, lock-her-in-a-tower nonsense when she needed it, Hope wondered desperately?

"She is the fairest in the land, and the keeper of my heart."

She'd given up trying to stop him, but he drew to a somewhat smug close now, so she guessed it was over.

Sonnet had been pushing it a bit then, she thought rather unkindly.

"Um, thank you." She smiled tightly. "That was, ah…"

"Interesting," Elodie came to the rescue, the embodiment of a mannerly lady. "So very interesting. I'm sure that Hope enjoyed it immensely."

"Oh. Yes, yes of course."

"Well, there is plenty more where that came from, Miss Templeworth," Alphonsus threatened. "Perhaps I might prevail upon you to join me in the gardens so that I can read more to you? I have a notebook filled with them."

Cheska's snort only increased Hope's irritation.

"Miss Templeworth, I believe the next is mine."

Hope could have wept with relief as Albert Truant appeared in front of her.

"Of course, it is, I had quite forgotten. Excuse me, won't you, Alphonsus?" she trilled as she practically dragged Albert's sizeable frame to the dancers already lining up. "Thank you again for the poem."

Dancing with Albert was a little akin to jumping from the frying pan into the fire. All the young ladies in Halton knew that when he got foxed, his hands had a tendency to wander. And he was a terribly clumsy dancer. But it was either endure this dance with him or endure a notebook filled with insipid rhymes. So, a trodden-on toe or two and a bit of overfamiliarity seemed the lesser of two evils.

Lord, what was she doing here? She was miserable. Who was her presence here helping? What was it achieving?

She went through the motions of the steps and somehow managed to keep up an inane conversation for the duration, but her mind was elsewhere. Somewhere far away in the vicinity of her heart. With a man she might not ever see again.

Suddenly it was too much, her feelings, her longing, her misery. And to her horror, Hope felt tears smart her eyes. Mercifully, the dance came to an end, and she managed to bob a quick curtsy before she turned and ran from the room. Not knowing or caring who saw.

She just needed to gather herself. That was all. Take a few minutes out and just endure for a little while longer. Except, she didn't want to. She wanted to be alone. She wanted to lick her wounds and cry and figure out how on earth she was supposed to get through another day without Gideon.

And so, knowing that she was going to be in a world of trouble, she turned and marched toward the gate at the end of the magistrate's garden and into the meadows beyond.

She knew this place like the back of her hand. She wasn't

afraid of the dark or of being alone here. And perhaps she was a glutton for punishment, but Hope found her feet steering her toward the lake. Toward where this madness had first begun.

She walked slowly, keeping an eye out for anyone who might give chase. Most likely Christian. Perhaps Sophia, who would no doubt try to make her own escape as soon as she noticed that Hope had given everyone the slip.

But she was alone. Painfully, tragically alone. She'd come back to the lake. Of course, she had. And she walked as close to the edge as she dared without getting her feet wet.

"Oh, for goodness' sake, Hope. Stop being so down in the doldrums."

She did wonder if it was a sign of madness that not only was she talking to herself, but she was *shouting* at herself in the middle of the night in an empty field.

"Do you usually have full-blown arguments with yourself in the middle of fields?"

The sound of Gideon's voice startled her, and she whipped around in time to see him smiling at her right before she lost her footing and fell backward into the freezing water.

"Damn it."

Gideon was torn between panic and laughter as Hope spun to face him with a screech, then tumbled into the lake.

He ran forward even as he acknowledged that perhaps sneaking up on her in the middle of the night hadn't been his cleverest idea. But he'd been so anxious to see her. Missed her so much that he'd known he wouldn't be able to rest until he saw her again.

She sat up coughing and spluttering, her hair now a sodden, tangled mess, her dress completely soaked. And he couldn't help it then, he burst into laughter at the sight of her. But he quickly remembered, it was no longer summer, and the temperature had cooled dramatically in the last few weeks.

The last thing he wanted was her getting cold. So, he waded in, grateful that he was still in his riding boots, and bent to fish her out.

"How nice of you to reenact our first meeting for my return." He grinned, unable to help himself as he scooped her into his arms. She wrapped her arms around his neck, and he winced slightly at the feel of the icy water now soaking through his clothing.

"I'm sorry, sweetheart," he said softly as he walked them both to the relative safety of the lake edge. "I didn't mean to startle and then almost drown you."

When she didn't laugh, he looked down into her face, concern slithering along his veins. He knew they had so much to talk about. Knew that he'd left in less than perfect circumstances. And perhaps joking and flirting weren't the correct approach to take.

He'd just been so happy to see her there, though he could wring her neck for wandering around alone in the middle of the night. He'd been on his way to the magistrate's party when he'd spotted her, knowing even from a distance that it was Hope.

"You shouldn't be out here alone," he said, his tone made severe by his worry for her.

"Why?" she drawled then. "In case some madman makes me fall in the lake?"

He gazed into her eyes and there it was. That spark of mischief. His heart squeezed at the sight.

"You came back," she whispered.

His throat grew inexplicably tight.

"I told you I would," he whispered right back.

And then his wild, beautiful, brazen Hope leaned up and kissed him.

Chapter Twenty-Seven

G IDEON WAITED ALL of two seconds before taking control of the kiss, his groan wrenched from his soul.

"I missed you," he confessed against her lips before plunging his tongue inside her mouth, dragging those maddening, breathless moans from her.

"I missed you," she said back, a shudder wracking her body. "I cannot believe it's really you."

Gideon allowed himself the indulgence of kissing her for a few seconds more before her trembling got the better of him.

"I need to get you out of these clothes," he said, and her eyes gleamed with such wickedness that he nearly dropped her there and then.

"Sounds wonderful," she purred, and he glared at her with mock severity even as his body lit up at everything she implied.

"I don't want you to catch cold," he tried again, feeling a little like a stern governess.

"Then why don't you warm me?" she asked, running a hand along her cheek.

He couldn't do it. He couldn't worry about her and resist her at the same time, especially not when she was pressed against him like this. And not when he knew they had so many serious things to discuss.

So, he set her gently on her feet, removing her hands from around his neck and taking a very large, deliberate step away from her.

"We need to talk," he said quietly as he reached up and undid his riding jacket.

He watched as she swallowed, her eyes tracking his movements.

"We do," she agreed.

"We need to get you home and dry. And then we need to talk," he reiterated, shrugging off his jacket.

This time, her only response was a nod. He prowled close enough to place his jacket on her shoulders.

And then because he couldn't resist touching her, because he knew he was free to do so unencumbered by his past or any complications, he reached out and stroked a finger along her cheek.

"How is it possible that you've grown more beautiful?"

Her snort wasn't a bit ladylike and was so very Hope that he grinned.

"Oh yes, I've always thought the drowned rat look was particularly attractive on me."

He could only laugh at her outrageousness, so happy to be back with her that the ache in his chest that had been his constant companion these past few weeks simply disappeared.

"I've always quite liked rats," he said as he turned and guided her toward his mount, wincing slightly at the sound of her soaking slippers hitting the gravel. "So, you're in luck."

She scowled up at him.

"To think I left behind an entire book of poetry dedicated to me for this," she sniffed.

A lance of possessive jealously shot through him as he reached out and grasped her waist.

"Someone's been writing a book of poetry about you?"

She rolled her eyes completely unperturbed by his envy.

"Someone is always writing poetry about me," she scoffed. "I was forced to listen to one of them this very evening, against my will."

He still wasn't happy about it, but she sounded so horrified that it appeased him somewhat. He lifted her onto the saddle, nearly expiring on the spot when she lifted her sodden skirts and threw one leg over the horse, so she was sitting astride, her thighs bared to his view.

"Are you trying to kill me?" he growled as he pulled himself up behind her, knowing by her gasp that she could feel exactly what the sight of those legs had done to him.

"I told you I missed you," he whispered in her ear before nipping at the lobe.

"Yet, you won't do anything to show me," she whispered as she leaned her head against his chest.

"Would you like me to recite poetry for you, sweetheart?"

"Wasn't drowning me punishment enough?"

Damn, she was incorrigible, Gideon told himself as he wrapped an arm around her waist and hurried the horse along. She was going to be a handful, no doubt about it.

HOPE HELD A finger to her lips to indicate that Gideon should be quiet before she slipped open the doors to the kitchen.

As she'd suspected, the room was empty at this time of night. The staff were used to retiring early when the family were out, knowing that the girls would help themselves to whatever they might want upon their return.

Mama never wanted anything except her bed when she came back from a party.

Hope opened the door at the exact angle needed to ensure it didn't squeak, then pulled Gideon through before shutting it again.

"Do I want to know how you know precisely how far to open that door without making a sound?" he asked under his breath.

"I don't know, do you?" she retorted, still hardly daring to believe that he was here with her.

"I don't think my heart could take it."

She was dying to know what had happened. He didn't seem troubled, but she couldn't begin to guess at why that would be. Was it because he was so happy to be a father? Or had he figured out a way for him to have his son and her in his life?

Either way, she'd already decided while he'd been gone that if he came back to her, she would support any endeavor, any plan if it meant she could be with him.

She led the way up the staircase, pointed out to him where to stand and where to avoid. Only when they were in her bedchamber, with the door safely locked behind them, did she breathe properly.

"The fact that you know exactly how to sneak in and out of this house terrifies me," he said softly. "But not as much as seeing you alone in a field in the middle of the night did."

She really did try to look contrite, but it obviously didn't work if his growl was anything to go by.

"I have to get out of these clothes," she said mostly to avoid an argument. His face turned predatory, his sudden smile, positively wolfish. "Are you going to turn around?" she asked.

"No."

She felt self-conscious, just as she had that day at the lake, and she knew that he was toying with her. Waiting to see how much she was willing to brazen it out. And since she'd rather die than ever back down from a challenge, she shrugged then set about undressing herself.

She got as far as reaching behind her to try and undo the buttons on the back of her gown when he was suddenly upon her, kissing her senseless.

"You win," he huffed before kissing her once again.

Oh, she could get used to this, Hope thought happily. She could have a lifetime of this, and it wouldn't be enough to keep her satisfied.

"We have to talk," he said even as he moved to trail kisses along her neck. "I have so much that I need to tell you."

She couldn't wait. She wanted him with a strength that honestly scared her. And while a part of her was desperate to know what had happened between him and the dowager countess, another part of her was terrified to find out. Terrified that it would further damage her mangled heart if he confessed that he was leaving for good this time. That he needed to marry that awful woman for the sake of the babe. That he would belong to someone else.

So, she put a hand on his chest, waiting while he lifted his head to gaze into her eyes.

"Are you going away again?" she asked.

His eyes softened, and he reached out to cup the nape of her neck, a thumb brushing over her cheek.

"Not without you," he said softly. "Never again without you."

And it was enough. For now, as the truth of his words seeped into her bones, it was enough.

"Then kiss me," she demanded, but he hesitated.

"There are things I must tell you, sweetheart," he said. "Important things."

"But you, you don't have to leave. You're not..." She could barely get the words out so fearful was she of the answer. "You don't have an understanding with Elaine?"

"No, Hope," he breathed. "I swore to you that I would only return when I'd made things right. I wouldn't lie to you."

She felt her pulse fluttering wildly with a mixture of nerves and acute joy. And she knew he must be able to feel it with his hand pressed against her neck.

"It's a bit of a mess." She really was doing her best to concentrate on what he was saying, but it wasn't easy. "The boy isn't mine, sweetheart."

Her heart stopped dead at the relief that swept through her.

"It took us an age to track her down. She'd run, you see, and we couldn't figure out why."

"Gideon. Tell me later," she said, and this time when she demanded that he kiss her, he happily obliged.

Chapter Twenty-Eight

T HE ONLY SOUNDS in the room were the ticking of the ormolu clock on the mantel and the crackling of the fire already dying down in the hearth. Hope knew that her abigail would have tended to it whilst lying out her night-rail that now lay draped across her crisp, white counterpane.

Hope had no idea why she was fixating on such tiny details. Not when Gideon was gazing at her with such wicked intent.

His hands moved from her face, sweeping down her back and then up again to undo the tiny, pearl buttons.

Gideon leaned down to nibble at the racing pulse of her throat.

"If you get sick, I'll never let you hear the end of it," he warned.

"If I get sick it will be because you made me fall in the lake," she gasped, hearing the breathlessness in her tone but unable to help it.

"If you hadn't been foolishly wandering around by yourself, I wouldn't have found you near the lake, and you couldn't have fallen into it," he groused against her neck.

She opened her mouth to deliver a scathing retort, but his deft fingers had loosened the last of her buttons, and he pulled the gown apart with a satisfied grunt.

Lifting his head, he watched her face as he pulled the material down her shoulders, then her waist, until it was a pool at her feet.

Wordlessly, he held out a hand and she grasped it, using him to balance as she stepped out of the dress and kicked it to the side.

Her maid would curse her to perdition, Hope knew. Not that it would be the first time.

She stood silent and trembling under his scrutiny. Hardly daring to breathe as he released her hand, then moved both of his to her sodden hair, she simply waited while he carefully removed the pins that had survived her unexpected late-night dip.

When her hair was loose, trailing down her back, those clever, wicked hands moved to the ties of her stays and made light work of divesting her of them. He stepped back and once again looked her over. The awe in his eyes, as though he couldn't quite believe that she was real, melted any reservations Hope might have had left, and she whispered his name, the sound broken and pleading.

She thought he might pull her to him, but instead, he reached out and trailed one, heated finger along her collarbone, then downward, tracing the hem of her shift, his lips quirking slightly at the path of gooseflesh he left in his wake.

"I've missed every inch of you," he said, his voice deep and smooth like the finest brandy. "I hardly know where to start."

When he finally moved, she could have wept with relief. But he didn't take her in his arms or even reach for her. To Hope's shock, he dropped to his knees in front of her. And then finally, *finally* his hands were on her waist as he leaned forward and pressed a kiss to her stomach, the heat of which seared her through the damp material of her chemise.

Her blood was so heated, her desire so potent, that she almost sobbed at even this briefest of touches.

He was so tall that even kneeling before her, his face was tantalizingly close to her aching breasts. She couldn't resist running a hand through his hair and tugging gently as though to guide that clever mouth toward them.

His laughter caressed her skin, causing yet another shudder to rack her body. "If you don't do something quickly, I'm going to expire."

He laughed again. But the eyes he lifted to her face were filled with devilish fire.

"Well, we can't have that, can we?" he asked before unleashing himself.

It was as if her words had broken the walls of his restraint and he reached up, pulling the chemise from her. And then his mouth was on her skin, his teeth and lips and tongue causing a conflagration sweeping through her while she held on and happily went up in the flames.

Hope wondered, somewhere in the still barely coherent back of her mind, if she should be concerned that he was still fully dressed save for his jacket, and she was completely naked, save for her stockings. But oh, she didn't care. Not while his teeth clamped onto a nipple at the same time as his thumb found that secret part of her, right at her core, which sent lightning shooting through her veins.

Her grip on his hair grew desperate, and she pushed against his hand, wanting more, wanting what she didn't know to ask for. He slipped a finger inside, groaning against her breast before moving to the other.

She could barely catch her breath past the pleasure that rippled through her as the first one, then another finger set a rhythm that was almost punishing in its sheer, uncontrollable bliss. And just when she thought she wouldn't be able to handle more, as she was begging and pleading through the storm brewing in her veins, he removed his mouth from her breast. Leaning back on his heels, he gave her one, wicked smile before leaning forward and replacing his thumb with that clever, sinful tongue.

Hope shattered, the twisting, churning ache that had been building and building suddenly letting loose, and she couldn't stifle her cry as she came undone in his arms.

Before she could gulp down some much-needed air, he was standing and lifting her into his arms, striding to the bed with near-feral intent. And as quickly as her hunger for him had been sated it rose again as she felt him pressed against her.

There was no part of her that was scared. No part of her that felt she should wait to join with him in every way possible.

He'd come back to her. And even if she didn't get forever with him, she knew she would never want it with anyone else. Knew that nobody would ever make her feel the way he did. And so, when he lay her on the bed, she wrapped her legs around his waist, pressing against him and reveling in the string of curses that fell from his lips as his hips surged against the very heart of her.

"Hope, I don't want to do this."

"I do," she said firmly, willing him to see the truth in her eyes. "I do want it. You. All of you."

She could see it in his face, that he was fighting against his body's urge, that he was trying to do the right thing. But as far as she was concerned, the only right thing was him. Them, together in every way imaginable.

"Please, Gideon," she whispered, and she saw the moment that her plea broke through the last of his defenses.

He reared up to pull his lawn shirt from his body, and she took a moment to simply drink in the incredible sight of him. He was a work of art, the finest sculpture of the gods come to life.

Her mouth dried as she took in the impossibly large shoulders, the bulging muscles of his forearms as he leaned over her, keeping his weight on his elbows. She ran her eyes down the ridges of his abdomen, further to the trail of hair that disappeared under his breeches.

And she couldn't help herself. She reached out to feel the hot, silken smoothness of his skin, the hard, unyielding muscle that covered every part of them. He hissed at the contact as though her touch burned, but he didn't move, just stayed perfectly still while she explored him.

Only the sweep of her hand against the hard length of him snapped that implacable stillness and he groaned, pushing himself against her open palm.

"I don't know what to do."

"You could have fooled me," he panted as though he were in pain. But she smiled with utter feline pride that she'd managed to reduce a man like Gideon to breathlessness.

Growing bolder, she dipped that same hand beneath the material of his breeches and this time, his gasp was accompanied by one of her own. She wrapped a hand around him, stroking the smooth, hard length of him, and would have continued in rapt fascination had he not suddenly reached down and stopped her with a hand around her wrist.

"That's enough of that," he growled, and for moment, she thought maybe she'd done something wrong, but the savage gleam in his eyes was enough to tell her that no, it would appear she'd done something very, very right.

Letting her go and standing at the foot of the bed, Gideon took seconds to divest himself of his boots and breeches until he was gloriously, unashamedly naked before her.

And taking in the length of him without the barrier of his clothes, Hope felt a tiny flickering of misgiving.

"Um." She licked her lips nervously as he once more lowered himself to the bed, gripping her knees to widen them and setting between her legs. "I-I'm not altogether sure you'll fit," she confessed.

But rather than seem concerned, he just looked utterly smug.

"I'm flattered that you think so, sweetheart," he quipped. "But trust me, I'll fit. You were made for me."

The words and the tenderness in them brought tears to her eyes, her heart filling with so many emotions it was impossible to even try to articulate them all. And so, what she couldn't speak, she tried to show by reaching up and pressing her lips to his own.

It was all the encouragement he needed to plunge his tongue inside her mouth and set to work bringing her body back to that dazzling cliff edge. And then, he was there, pushing slowly, carefully against her inch by torturous inch.

He felt foreign and huge but so incredibly good that Hope

couldn't stop herself from rolling her hips, and with one, final thrust, he was seated inside her.

She winced at the discomfort. Not pain, not exactly. But it wasn't entirely pleasant.

A small whimper slipped from her mouth, but he was there pressing loving, teasing kisses on her lips, at her throat, nibbling wickedly at her ear.

"You feel perfect, sweetheart," he whispered as he began to move inside her, and with every thrust, the discomfort was replaced with sheer, utter bliss. "You *are* perfect."

Her need grew unbearable, and she moved her hips against him once more, her legs wrapping around him to pull him deeper, her nails clawing at his back. And the actions seemed to make him wild. His movements grew harder, faster until he pushed her over that edge, and she shot higher than she ever had before, rejoicing as she felt him fly with her.

Hope had to bite his shoulder to keep from crying out and waking the household, while he buried his own shout of release in her hair.

And as she floated back to earth, gloriously, wonderfully sated, he lifted his head to stare into her eyes.

"Hope," he said, brushing a lock of sweat-dampened hair from her face.

"Hmm?" she couldn't even stir herself to move, her body feeling like liquid beneath his.

"I love you."

Chapter Twenty-Nine

GIDEON WATCHED CAREFULLY as Hope's eyes widened at his words and then her mouth widened in the most beautiful smile he'd ever seen, those dimples that he'd lost sleep over making an appearance.

She was staring at him in wonder, yet how could she not know? He would never have taken the gift of her innocence if he hadn't planned to marry her. If he didn't know that she was all he'd ever want, every second of every day.

The sex had been life-altering. He was well aware of what an honor it was for him to be the one to introduce her to the art of lovemaking, but he should have known she would need no real instruction. She was a natural. And she had ruined him.

He'd never felt anything like what had just happened here. Even now, his cock twitched in anticipation of a repeat.

She lifted a hand and cupped his cheek as her mouth opened, and he held his breath, his heart straining, waiting desperately to hear her say she loved him.

The sound of a door slamming open rattled through the house.

Damn it. He'd forgotten about her bloody family. They both listened, frozen in place, as laughter, shouting, and enough choice words to turn a sailor's ears blue floated up the stairs toward Hope's bedroom.

"That girl has gone quite too far this time," Mrs. Templeworth's voice rang out, and she didn't sound best pleased.

He looked down at Hope, who only shrugged as if her mother being up in the boughs about her was an everyday occurrence. And he could only imagine that it was.

"Bad enough that I had to haul Sophia back inside. But Sir Alphonsus was searching for Hope for an age. He was quite put out."

"I think you'll find that *I* hauled Sophia back inside." This from Elodie whose calm tones were a direct contrast to Mrs. Templeworth's nasally complaints.

"Yes, thank you for that," Sophia's sarcasm was obvious even from up here.

Gideon didn't feel even remotely comfortable listening to this while he was still naked in Hope's bed, so he reluctantly withdrew, promising himself that he'd have them married and ensconced somewhere very private—and very far from Halton— by the month's end.

Moving as silently as he could, he hurried to at least put on his pants, turning in time to catch Hope brazenly ogling him. He quirked a brow, wondering if she'd be embarrassed, but of course, he should have known better and his blood stirred again as she raised a brow right back, a saucy smile curving her lips.

"Mother, did you even *hear* those Godforsaken poems?" That biting tone could only be the indomitable Francesca. "I don't blame her for running away. Nobody deserves to have that nonsense spouted at them."

Christ, they were loud, he thought distractedly, trying very much to ignore the fact that Hope was still naked in that bed with only the sheet covering her from the view.

"She only has to marry him, Cheska. Not listen to him."

Both Gideon and Hope froze at Mrs. Templeworth's statement. And a furious possessiveness had Gideon almost marching down there and setting them all straight. The only person Hope was marrying was him. If she wanted poetry, he'd read her some damned poetry.

She must have seen how angry he'd grown, for she leaned forward to whisper conspiratorially. "I wouldn't take that too seriously. Mama is always threatening to marry me off. It hasn't worked yet."

God, he loved her. Loved how stoutly she refused to be influenced into doing something she didn't want. Loved how she didn't take anything too seriously. And he especially loved that she'd defied her mother's attempts to get her wed.

"She's probably in raptures at the idea that I could be a baroness."

"A countess wouldn't do for her?" he asked quietly, watching her face.

The delicate pinkening of her cheeks was a thing of beauty, and he realized just how much he enjoyed knowing he could still make her blush.

Before she could answer, Francesca's voice sounded again.

"If you think she'll marry that oaf, I'll think you've been at the punch, Mother. You have to know she only means to marry Lord Claremont."

Once again, the air in the room seemed to freeze, and Gideon's heart hammered as he awaited Mrs. Templeworth's reply.

"That's all well and good, dear," the woman whined. "But he's run off, hasn't he? To God knows where. Thrown her over. To think she could have been a countess."

"I don't think he's thrown her over," Lady Brentford interjected gently, yet mercifully still loud enough for Gideon to hear.

"He hasn't," Cheska said stoutly. "He wouldn't. At least, I don't think he would."

"No, I don't think so either." This from Sophia Templeworth. "The way he looked at her was positively sickening."

Thankfully, he'd already confessed his feelings to Hope, Gideon thought wryly. Since her family were doing a good job of making him sound like an utter sop. But there was a warm feeling in his chest as he listened to them champion them, defend him, and believe in him. He didn't care that he'd made his love for their sister so obvious. And, he realized with a start, he was even looking forward to having them as sisters. Though he might need to speak to Brentford about keeping them on a leash. For his own peace of mind, if nothing else.

He'd thrown on his still-damp lawn shirt and made quick work of shoving on his creased riding jacket. His waistcoat and cravat he'd shirked hours ago on his mad dash back to Hope, so they were presumably still in the saddlebag of his horse.

His horse! The one he'd quickly shoved into an empty stall in the Templeworth stables. He turned to ask Hope if there was a way to get to the stables, and the horse, before anyone noticed. Listening with one ear as Sophia Templeworth still chattered away.

"He's as bad as Christian, all moon-eyed and looking at them as though they're something to eat."

"Who's as bad as me?"

Oh, why not, thought Gideon. *Let's throw Brentford into the mix, too.*

"And why," the deep, booming voice continued, "is there a strange horse in the stables?"

"THE TRICK IS not to panic," Hope whispered, tightening the belt of the robe she'd quickly donned as Gideon stared dubiously out the window. "Honestly, I've done it hundreds of times. Confidence is key."

She gave him a hearty slap of encouragement on the back, but it didn't seem to help, for he merely gave her a long-suffering look before turning his attention outside once more.

"It's a long drop," he said doubtfully. "And that branch is not going to hold my weight."

"Of course, it will," she said, though she was starting to doubt it herself. "Like I said, I've used it often. Probably more than the front door, actually."

"Yes, but I'm significantly bigger than you," he pointed out as though she were a dimwit.

But he was right, she thought as her eyes wandered over those shoulders, those arms that had held her so tightly. The muscled thighs that had rubbed against her own with all that delicious friction that her body was still a little sore from.

She looked back up from her inappropriate musings to see him staring at her, one brow quirked as though he knew exactly where her thoughts had gone.

"Get your mind out of the gutter, woman," he griped, though he didn't sound particularly unhappy about it. "And help me come up with an escape plan that won't end in my death."

She contemplated the drop.

"Well, Christian can't kill you if you're already dead," she supplied unhelpfully.

He snorted in a way that implied he wasn't sure Christian could kill him anyway.

"Yes, but I can't marry you if I'm dead either, can I?"

He didn't miss the way her breath caught at her words.

"Y-you want to marry me?" she asked, her eyes shining. And he was struck dumb by her all over again. But he remembered himself enough to answer.

"Of course, I want to marry you," he said softly. "I love you. I don't want to spend a moment without you. I want to marry you and have babies with you and continue to have my whole world revolve around you since it already does. But again, I cannot do that if I die falling out of a tree."

He'd kept his tone deliberately light, aware that he still hadn't even had a chance to explain things with Elaine to her. But she threw her arms around him, nearly sending them both toppling out the window in the process. And Gideon had to sit on the ledge and wrap his arms around her to keep her safe.

"I love you, too," she burst out, her smile like a beam of sunshine. "I love you so much, Gideon. And I want all those things with you."

"So then, you'll settle for countess over baroness?" he drawled, leaning back against the window frame and pulling her to stand between his legs, escaping quite forgotten in the face of hearing those words from her and knowing that she was going to be his. Forever.

"If I must," she sighed.

"I promise to shower you with so many luxuries that you won't mind being a countess."

"Good," she purred. "Because as we both know, I only agreed to marry you for your money and title."

"You are an absolute tearaway." He nipped at her neck. "Don't remind me of what a blackguard I was. Anyway, I'm not even sure I'd care anymore if that were the only reason you agreed to be my wife. I'm so utterly besotted that I'd take you any way I could get you."

He allowed himself a brief grin at her cheekiness before bending to take her mouth in a sweet kiss. Unsurprisingly, as soon as their lips touched, his lust exploded, and he was just preparing to carry her back to bed, consequences be damned, when an unmerciful boom sounded and the door burst open, lock splintered to smithereens, to reveal a murderous looking Brentford and a gaggle of Templeworths, all standing in the hallway.

Chapter Thirty

ALL RIGHT.

Hope had been in some sticky situations in her lifetime. But she had never been caught trying to throw a man out her bedroom window. Which was precisely what she'd panicked and done when Christian had come flying into the room.

She'd screeched and jumped away from Gideon and then *tried to shove him out the window.* Thankfully, he'd had the sense to grab onto the wooden frame and stop himself from plunging to the ground below.

Even now, huddled with her sisters outside Papa's study, she couldn't quite believe that she'd almost killed him before she'd even had the chance to marry him.

She clutched the tumbler of brandy that Cheska had pressed into her hands, grateful that her three sisters sat with her as they all listened to the mumbled conversation from behind the study door.

"Lord, Elle. I never realized how excruciating it must have been for you when Philip Harrison was in there threatening to marry you," she whispered, remembering how Christian's cousin had indeed come and offered for her. It was that offer, and Papa's acceptance of it, that had set Elle's escape into motion.

"Well, at least it's the man you *want* in there." Elodie reached over to pat her hand comfortingly. "And nobody's going to object to the Earl of Claremont, are they? Especially since, well, since…"

"Since he was caught half-naked jumping out your window?" Cheska supplied helpfully.

"He was *not* half-naked," Hope objected. "Not then. And in his defense, I pushed him out the window."

"I'm glad you didn't succeed for what it's worth, Hope." Sophia smiled from the other side of her. "I quite like him."

The meeting seemed to be going on forever, though everything sounded like it had calmed down a bit at least.

For a while there she'd truly worried that Christian and Gideon were going to come to blows, and only Elodie's stepping between them had stopped it. But then, of course, Mama had started her hysterics and had awoken the entire household, including Papa, who'd actually deigned to leave his bedchamber to check on the commotion.

There'd been more screeching from Mama, and threats of bodily harm from Christian, and shouts of scandalized delight from her sisters.

And through it all, Gideon had just looked at her. Calmly and without a care in the world. And smiled.

As she sat here now, Hope kept the memory of that smile in her heart. He hadn't looked scared or worried. He'd just looked, well, happy. And she was happy, too. Or she would be when all of this nonsense was sorted out.

The only sounds now from the study were the odd, masculine rumbles. But nothing that sounded aggressive or life-threatening. Even Mama's sniffles and wailings had become the definite sounds of acceptance.

Hope and her sisters grew quiet as the meeting went on and on until, eventually, Sophia's and Cheska's heads dropped to each of her shoulders, their deep breathing indicating that they'd drifted off. A glance to the side showed that Elodie, too, was sleeping. Her head on Cheska's shoulder.

All the servants had been sent back to bed, and so Hope sat there in the quiet and the dark, listening to her sisters' deep breaths and knowing that she would never be able to sleep. Not when she knew her future, her entire happiness, was being discussed within that room.

GIDEON SIGHED AS he finally stood up and shook hands with both Mr. Templeworth, who he still had absolutely no respect for, and Brentford, for whom his respect had grudgingly grown.

After all, Christian had pointed out, when Gideon married Hope and shared the burden of big brother, he, too, would want to kill the man who snuck around the girls' bedchambers in the dark of night.

"It sort of takes you by surprise," Christian had confided quietly as they nursed tumblers of brandy and frowned when Templeworth, who'd shown a vague interest in the night's events, asked if he was planning on marrying Hope, explained the terms of her modest dowry, and then promptly fallen asleep at his desk. Even the man's odious wife had eventually passed out, her snores rumbling around the room and pushing the feather hanging off her turban up and down with each breath. "The protectiveness. The love for them. I truly do want the best for them all. And I truly would have happily killed you if you weren't so in love with her."

"I'm glad to hear it," Gideon had answered softly. And he meant it. He was glad Hope had someone who wanted the best for her. And he was glad to share in the responsibility of taking care of the younger two who might very well turn out to be the most difficult.

Christian chuckled softly and pinched the bridge of his nose. "I can't decide if I want our baby to be a girl just like her mother and aunts, or a boy so I don't go prematurely grey," he'd said, and as Gideon had offered his congratulations and sympathies for the viscount's plight, he couldn't help but think of Hope, her body rounded with his babe, looking at him with those doe eyes.

"Well," Christian had knocked back the entire contents of his glass and stood, with Gideon following suit, "I'm glad to have a fellow man-at-arms." He'd grinned as he'd moved around to shake awake Mr. and Mrs. Templeworth. "Though I daresay, you've had quite the introduction into the family fold."

"It's been absolute madness," he'd answered baldly.

"It usually is where the sisters are concerned. But what fun is midsummer without a little madness to go with it?"

Mr. Templeworth had come awake long enough to shake Gideon's hand and stagger off to his bedchamber, his wife practically sleepwalking in his wake.

Utterly useless, Gideon thought as he watched them. If Hope gave him daughters, he knew he'd be getting to work on that tower he'd threatened her with.

He followed Christian out of the room and stopped at the sight of the four sisters, heads bent toward each other and hands gripping each other even in repose. And he couldn't stop his smile at the sight, noticing that the viscount wore a matching one.

"I'm glad they have each other," he whispered, though he couldn't remove his eyes from Hope.

From his peripheral, he saw the viscount lean down and run a thumb along the dark-haired viscountess's cheek. "Me, too," he'd said, keeping his own adoring gaze on his wife.

Brentford quite clearly had it as bad as Gideon did. But he found he didn't mind having even more in common with the man, thinking it highly likely that they'd become fast friends, as well as brothers of a sort.

He watched as Christian gently shook first Francesca, then Sophia awake, watched as they blinked up at Christian, and then almost as one, turned assessing, identical blue gazes on him.

"Is it all sorted out then?" Francesca asked, her voice husky with sleep.

"Are you marrying Hope?"

He couldn't contain his smile at Sophia's question.

"I am," he said quietly.

"Oh marvelous," Cheska sighed. "Another domineering man trying to order us about." But he caught the glint of approval in her eyes and bowed deeply. "I shall try my utmost not to get too much in your way," he swore gallantly. She rolled her eyes at his words but smiled at him as she strode by him toward the family sleeping quarters.

Sophia stood and faced him.

"Will you let me ride that stallion of yours?" she demanded.

He looked to Christian, who gave him a quick, subtle nod. "First thing tomorrow," he answered and sighed in relief as she beamed at him, and he realized he'd passed some sort of test.

"'Night then," she called as she trailed after her sister.

Christian bent and swept his still-dozing wife into his arms. "I take it I can leave Hope in your capable hands?" he said as Elodie nuzzled into his neck.

"You trust me that much?" he asked, even as he relished the idea of getting to hold her again.

"Of course," Christian said as he walked toward the stairs with a determination that Gideon didn't want to dwell on, before calling over his shoulder. "I broke the lock, didn't I? So how much damage could you do?"

Chapter Thirty-One

HOPE STIRRED AT the feel of cool sheets under her back and a gentle kiss at her brow.

"Shh, sweetheart. Go back to sleep."

That was Gideon's voice. She gasped and came fully awake as she remembered. The locked door, the commotion, the meeting with her father.

She sprang into a sitting position to see that he was already on the bed facing her.

"Gideon, what happened?" She blinked rapidly, trying to clear her sleep-addled mind.

"It's all right, Hope. Everything is fine. Better than fine. And I can explain it all in the morning."

"No, no. Tell me now."

He sighed with exaggerated patience as he toyed with a lock of her hair.

"When we're wed, are you going to argue with me at every turn like this?"

"Probably," she answered swiftly. Then his words sank in.

"So, it went well then? There aren't any bullet holes in you," she continued, running a careful gaze over his body. "No bruises marring that pretty face."

He snorted even as he shook his head.

"No holes, no bruises. No problems. We are officially engaged, and I am now officially a man with a mission. To get you to an altar as fast as humanly possible."

His words were the most beautiful sound in the world, and she threw her arms around him, burying her face in his neck as tears of overwhelming joy threatened.

"What's the rush?" she sniffed, inhaling this intoxicating scent. Sandalwood and bergamot and something that was uniquely Gideon.

"The rush is that I want you alone away from your wonderful but slightly crazy family. A house filled with door locks that don't easily break."

She stifled her giggle against his neck before pulling back to stare into his black-as-sin eyes.

"I suppose Christian is keeping watch from the landing?"

"Christian is, if I'm not mistaken, currently engaged in activities that I would very much like you and I to be engaged in."

She caught his meaning straight away.

"Well, what's stopping you?" she purred, delighting in his agonized moan.

"A door that doesn't bloody well lock," he growled, pressing his forehead against her own. "And a house full of interfering relatives."

He kissed her then, taking his sweet time and driving her slowly mad. And when she was panting, when he seemed satisfied that he'd made her suffer as much as he was, he pulled away.

"Sleep, my Hope," he said as he stood. "Dream of me as I'll dream of you. And then tomorrow, at the lake, we can talk everything through. Get to work on that future of ours."

She lay back, doing as she was told for probably the first time in her life. And he leaned down to press a kiss against her brow.

"I love you," he whispered. "Beyond sense or reason. I love you."

"I love you," she said.

As it turned out, she didn't dream of him since that kiss of his made sure she wouldn't be able to sleep a wink.

But the next day, she was more than ready to have that talk.

GIDEON PACED AS he waited impatiently for Hope to arrive. The day was crisp and bright, but there was a coolness that proved summer was well and truly over.

He should be home now, he knew, overseeing the harvest like he'd planned. But home had become wherever Hope was. There was no chance of procuring a special license, he now knew having woken Kit and interrogated him about it. The trip to London would take too long and besides, he wanted to give Hope the opportunity to have the wedding she wanted.

Aunt and Uncle Bell had been told this morning of his betrothal. Uncle Bell's felicitations had been sincere, Aunt Bell's, less so. But given that they'd left Halton that morning and Gideon would be leaving soon afterward, he'd decided not to make too big a deal of it.

A twig snapped behind him, and he turned to see her sweep between the branches of the willow.

He hadn't grown accustomed to her beauty, he realized as his heart thundered. He likely never would. And it wasn't just how beautiful she was on the surface. But how beautiful her soul was. Her heart.

He wondered if she might be feeling a bit shy after what had happened between them last night. After all, she hadn't really had the chance to process it before all hell had broken loose. Neither had he. But it had been her first time, and he had wanted so much to be able to hold her and take care of her. To show her and tell her just how honored he was by such a gift, how happy she made him just by being nearby.

But the smile she trained on him was anything but shy as she launched herself at him and threw herself into his arms, squealing in delight as he lifted her from her feet and took her mouth in a blazing kiss.

He hadn't felt so joyous, so carefree in years. Perhaps ever. But like so much else in his life, Hope had changed that.

Carefully setting her on her feet, he reached out and grabbed her hand, relishing the fact that he could.

"Come," he said, pulling her gently toward the rock where he'd set a picnic of champagne and apple tarts, which he'd learned from a helpful Sophia were Hope's favorites. Well, "helpful" might have been a stretch since she'd only agreed to tell him once she was atop his horse.

He'd held true to his word just that morning and brought Apollo over to the Templeworth stables. Admittedly, he'd been hoping to catch a glimpse of Hope, but he'd only found Sophia back in her usual uniform of breeches and a white shirt, her hair plated haphazardly.

He'd been a little concerned about her rather tiny frame on his mountainous stallion but that had quickly turned to shock and then awe. She had the best seat he'd ever seen, and she was as comfortable on the mount than she was on the ground.

It had taken her only seconds to fall in love with Apollo and only seconds more to blatantly use the horse to blackmail all sorts of information out of her.

"I take it Sophia told you of my penchant for apple tarts." She beamed as she took in the simple display.

Gideon couldn't stop himself from touching her, lifting their linked hands so he could place a kiss on the back of hers. He guided her to sit, remembering with perfect clarity just what they'd gotten up to the first time they'd come here. From the blush staining her cheeks, he guessed Hope was remembering, too. And he found himself having to have a stern word with his body about how new to all this she was. How sore she might be.

"How are you feeling?" he asked with no small measure of concern as he handed her a glass of frothy champagne.

"Overwhelmed," she admitted with endearing honesty. "So much has happened in such a short space of time. I'm quite reeling from it, truth be told."

"You don't regret it, do you?" he asked, suddenly terrified that he'd somehow brow-beat her into something she wasn't sure of. A lot *had* happened, between them yes but also with Elaine and the confusion she'd caused with her damned scheming.

Before he could work himself into a proper panic, however, Hope leaned forward and grabbed his hand. "I have no regrets, Gideon," she said, her face open and filled with a contented sincerity. "I love you. And I want nothing more than to marry you."

"Thank God," he breathed, squeezing her hand as relief swept through him. "I don't think I could have stood it if you'd wanted to cry off."

"Cry off?" She laughed, scrambling over with no hesitation and burrowing herself against his side. Christ, he loved that she was so tactile, so open with her affections. He wrapped an arm around her and simply held her close, breathing in the fresh meadow scent of her hair and skin.

True happiness. That's what this was. Unadulterated love and happiness.

"Are you mad? Even if either of us wanted to, there's no stopping it now. My mother has the chance to be connected to the mighty Claremonts. There's no getting away. You're stuck forever, whether you like it or not."

He pressed a kiss against the top of her head.

"It's a good thing I like it then, isn't it?" he drawled.

They sat in contented silence for a while before she stirred, sitting up and turning to face him, her lavender skirts spread around her feet.

"Did you talk? With your stepmother, I mean. Is she gone?"

"Yes and no," he answered wanting only honesty between them. And he figured that before they got onto far more pleasant subjects, they needed to lay that particular ghost to rest. So, taking her hand in his, he told her everything.

Chapter Thirty-Two

HOPE HAD LISTENED silently whilst Gideon had told her about the entire sorry tale around his stepmother and her poor, innocent babe.

She didn't stir at all until he turned worried eyes on her.

"I never thought to ask," he said quietly. "If such an arrangement would be acceptable to you. I understand, after everything she's done, after she nearly cost me you, that it seems foolhardy to help her. Believe me, I couldn't care less about her. But that boy…"

He shook his head, and Hope's heart twisted in response.

"It didn't feel right not to try and give him a fighting chance. But if it makes you in any way uncomfortable, I understand."

"Gideon, stop," she interrupted gently. "I couldn't be happier that you did what you did for young Charles," she assured him. "Lady Claremont, I'd love nothing more than to scratch her eyes out. And I can't pretend I'd ever be relaxed in her presence. But you didn't want to turn away from a child in need. Why would I ever think that anything less than wonderful? It is a testament to your good heart, your kind soul. The very things I love you for."

He sighed in obvious relief as though he'd been holding his breath waiting to see what she'd say. And she realized that, had she asked him to, he would have made himself unhappy by ending the arrangement he'd made with Elaine. Would have lived with the guilt of such a thing just to give her what she wanted.

She'd known, of course, that she was lucky in her choice of husband. But to see the evidence so clearly in his eyes? It was a heady feeling, indeed.

"I have to admit, though, even if it makes me wicked, that I am glad you're not tied to her in any way."

"Believe me, nobody is happier about that than I," he assured her. "And as for being wicked, Hope, darling, you know that's one of my favorite things about you."

Just like that, the air became charged with that *frisson* that always seemed to crackle around them. Her heart began fluttering wildly, and he reached out to press a hand against her erratic pulse.

"Are you sore?" he asked softly. "From last night?"

Hope could feel her cheeks heating at the frank question, but she held his stare, knowing it was only concern for her that made him ask.

"A little," she answered. "But not enough to put me off further activities."

His smile was the face of a fiend, and he leaned forward, gently tipping her back until she was lying on the blanket beneath him.

"What sort of activities did you have in mind then?" he asked, pressing softly maddening kisses along her neck and jaw.

"Oh, I don't know," she teased. "I'm so new to all of this. But you know what they say, practice makes perfect."

He pulled his head back to gaze down at her, a world of love on his face and in his eyes.

"You're already perfect, sweetheart," he said. "Believe me, you don't need any practice."

"Well, in that case, maybe you could read me some of that poetry you promised?" She quirked a brow as though waiting for him to become the Bard reincarnate.

He frowned down at her for a moment before clearing his throat.

"*An Ode to My Lady of the Lake,*" he intoned dramatically. And before he'd even got past the first sentence of utter gibberish, she was laughing so hard, she couldn't breathe.

"*There was a young lady who lived by the lake.*

Who swam with the carp and the eels and the hake…"

"Stop," she begged, gasping for breath. "I love a great many things about you, Gideon Bell. But your way with words isn't one of them."

He had the audacity to look mightily affronted for a moment before that achingly exciting gleam appeared in his eyes.

"Perhaps I should put my mouth to better use, then," his voice dripped with promise, and it was all Hope could do to nod and wrap her arms around his neck.

"Yes," she whispered. "Perhaps you should."

Chapter Thirty-Three

THE BELLS RANG out among the small churchyard of Halton, and its residents couldn't quite believe that Hope Templeworth had finally married.

In the three months since the betrothal had been announced, they'd all shamelessly taken bets on whether or not she'd lose interest in the handsome earl and move to someone new. The people who'd known her the longest, however, had known that there was something different about Lord Claremont. And Miss Hope was different around him, too. She'd been truly happy in his presence. And truly miserable when she'd been parted from him while the banns had been read every month by his brother, Reverend Bell.

She'd moped around Halton while he'd gone off to oversee things at his main seat and prepare it for the arrival of his new countess.

And again, the betting started. Some thought she would return to type and flirt outrageously with any and every poor, unsuspecting male in the vicinity. Those people were soon parted with their coin, for she had been unusually subdued, even downright miserable until the earl had finally come back for their wedding.

On one thing, everyone in Halton could agree, she was the single most beautiful bride anyone had ever seen. And when she'd left the church on the arm of her smiling husband, it was obvious by the look of dazed devotion in his eyes that he agreed with the sentiment.

They walked past their smiling families and did their best to ignore the weeping baron who kept trying to shout poetry at her until the Viscount Brentford had practically carried the man from the churchyard.

But the stunning bride and her husband had just laughed, holding on to each other as though they'd never let go.

Nobody hung around too long, as snowflakes began to dance around their heads. But the whole village had been invited back to Templeworth Manor to continue the festivities, so the bride and groom were soon blissfully alone as they meandered to the earl's carriage, in no rush to join their guests.

"I still think my poem was better than his." Gideon sulked as he handed Hope into the plush interior of his carriage and climbed in behind her.

A quick rap on the ceiling had them trundling along toward the manor house. And as soon as they were on the move, Gideon closed over the blue velvet curtains, shielding them from prying eyes, then reached over and lifted his bride onto his lap, groaning in satisfaction as she straddled him, a wicked grin on her face.

His bride.

He still couldn't quite believe it. Just as he couldn't quite believe how truly ethereal she looked today in ice-white satin. Sparking diamonds at her ears and throat, and in the tiara she wore.

She looked like an angel. And he knew that he'd spend his life wondering how he'd gotten so lucky, what he'd done to deserve her.

Her mother had spared no expense on the gown, Hope had written him during their time apart when the only things that had stopped him going mad from missing her were those humorously biting letters. She had had to be stopped from painting "my daughter is a countess" on the front door, Hope had written.

He'd assumed she was joking until Elodie, her stomach softly rounded, had laughingly confirmed it when he'd visited the family as soon as he'd set foot back in Halton.

Elodie and Christian had gone home for a couple of months but had traveled back for the wedding. They would leave the following day, as would Hope and Gideon. But while Elodie and Christian were returning to his Surrey estate, Gideon was taking Hope to Europe for a month.

Just the idea of having her completely to himself had him hardening beneath her.

"And I still think," she leaned down to drop a sweet, seductive kiss on his mouth, "That you do much better work with this mouth of yours when you're not speaking."

Christ, she'd be the death of him. He'd had no time alone with her in the week since he'd returned to stay at the rectory with Kit. When he did catch a glimpse of her in the midst of the panicked wedding planning, she almost always had a sister or her mother in toe.

But now. Now it was just her. And just him. And nobody to disturb them.

"You have no idea the things I've dreamed about doing with this mouth, wife," he whispered in her ear, laughing softly as she whimpered in response.

"Well..." She sat up just long enough to untie his black breeches. "Are you going to keep talking about it, or are you going to show me?"

He dragged her face down to his in a punishing kiss, delving his tongue inside her mouth as he positioned her above him. It was wild, uninhibited, and probably not the right way to start a marriage, but he was so desperate for her, and she didn't seem to care.

In fact, she seemed equally eager as she moaned into his mouth just as his hips surged up to fuse them together.

"This is madness," she panted.

"When has there been anything *but* madness between us?" he quipped in response.

He felt the telltale tightening of her core just before she went over the edge, and he held her close as he followed her into the abyss, both of them clinging on for dear life. Gideon seeing literal stars behind his eyelids.

It took him a moment to come back down to earth.

And even longer to realize that the carriage had stopped.

Hope seemed to realize it, too, for she lifted her head from his chest and groaned. Not in pleasure but in pain at the afternoon they were going to have to endure.

He looked into her beautiful face, studied her for a moment, then nodded his head firmly.

Positioning her back on the bench across from his, he reached forward and cracked open the carriage door. And after a brief, quiet chat with his driver, he closed it and they were moving again.

Hope frowned in confusion.

"Where are we going?" she asked. "The celebration is on in the Manor House."

"I decided to take a page out of the Hope Templeworth, now Lady Claremont, Book of Bad Behavior." He shrugged.

"Did you now?" she asked haughtily. "And what page might that be?"

"The page that says as long as we have each other, we shouldn't give a damn what's expected of us and that we should do what we want."

"So, page four then," she quipped, and he laughed, elation zinging through him.

"Indeed." He nodded sagely as though either of them were making any sense.

"Page four. Don't be afraid to run away from one's wedding and go instead to the lake where you found true, unending love."

Her eyes began to glisten at his words, and damned if he didn't feel a lump of emotion in his own throat.

"My mother will be at the smelling salts for weeks," she warned him.

"Page five," he continued as the carriage pulled to a stop. "Your mother can't get us in Paris."

Her peal of laughter sounded as he jumped out of the conveyance, then reached up to lift her from it, taking his sweet time in letting her slide down his body.

Even after their wild coupling of moments ago, he wanted her again.

"This is madness," she repeated the words she'd breathed when she'd been writhing about him.

"Just like when we met. Sheer madness between us as always," he repeated his own words. "Although at least the midsummer madness that brought us together was warmer."

Indeed, their warm breath clouded the air between them, but the look his countess turned on him could have melted the very ground around them.

"Well, then." She leaned into him, and he felt every delicious curve of her body beneath her fur-lined white cloak. "I suppose my very clever but not quite poetic husband will just have to think of a way to heat me up, won't he?"

And so, he did.

About the Author

Nadine Millard is an international best-selling author hailing from Dublin, Ireland.

Having studied and then worked in law for a number of years, Nadine began to live her dream of writing when she had the first of her three children.

She released her debut novel in 2014 and has been writing ever since.

When she's not writing she can be found reading anything she can get her hands on, ferrying her three children to school and clubs, spoiling her cat, her dog, and snatching time with her long-suffering husband!

You can find out all about Nadine and her books at www.nadinemillard.com.